BEYOND GOOD AND EVIL:
THE ETERNAL SPLIT-SECOND SOUND-LIGHT BEING

By

BRAD BLANTON

OTHER BOOKS BY BRAD BLANTON

RADICAL HONESTY: How to Transform Your Life by Telling the Truth

PRACTICING RADICAL HONESTY: How to Complete the Past, Live in the Present and Build a Future with a Little Help from Your Friends

RADICAL PARENTING: Seven Steps To a Functional Family in a Dysfunctional World

HONEST TO GOD: A Change of Heart that Can Change the World

THE TRUTHTELLERS: Stories of Success by Radically Honest People

The New Revised Edition of Radical Honesty

Sparrowhawk Publications
Stanley, Virginia
Text and Cover Design by Victoria Valentine
Printed by United Graphics, Inc.
Printed in the United States of America
Published simultaneously in Canada
June 2005

ISBN: 0-9706938-5-0

*Dedicated to all the people in the world
who have paid enough attention
to their experience of being here
to get to the place Rumi refers to when he says
"there is a field, out beyond good and evil.
I will meet you there."*

O sweet spontaneous
earth how often have
the
doting
fingers of
prurient philosophers pinched
and
poked
thee
has the naughty thumb
of science prodded
thy
beauty. How
often have religions taken
thee upon their scraggy knees
squeezing and
buffeting thee that thou mightiest conceive
gods
but
true
to the incomparable
couch of death thy
rhythmic lover
thou answerest them
only
with
Spring

—e.e. cummings

contents

EDITOR'S PREFACE

WHAT I HAVE PUT TOGETHER HERE, under one cover, is a book composed of three parts: (1) a condensed version of a short book written by Victor Myerson, M.D., psychiatrist, (2) a book review of that book written by Peter Howard, Ph.D., Clinical Psychologist, and (3) the transcript of one television show, *The Dick Cavett Show*, where Drs. Myerson and Howard appeared together earlier this year. I have labeled these three parts "Book I, Book II and Book III." They are all about the same person, Peter Howard, but different people wrote them, before being edited by me. Their titles and subject matter are as follows:

Book I is my condensation of *The Case of Peter X: A Modern Day Approach to Paranoid Schizophrenia with Delusions of Grandeur,* which was written by Dr. Victor Myerson, and first published four years ago.

Book II is a review of Dr. Myerson's book, which appeared in *The New York Review of Books* a few years back. This review is titled "The Eternal Split-Second Sound-Light Being" and was written by Dr. Peter Howard. In the review Peter Howard admits that he himself is Peter X, the subject of the book by Dr. Myerson.

Book III is a transcription of *The Dick Cavett Show, A Special Retrospective Event,* done in March of this year, and it describes the confrontation between Drs. Howard and Myerson on that television show. Each of these books is an elaboration of the same picture. The picture is a time exposure of a man who, floundering in an ocean of suggestions, may, or may not, have discovered the Gulf Stream.

intR⊙DuctioN

I AM EDITING THIS BOOK because I very much identify with the person this book is about. He and I have reached many of the same conclusions. If I could speak to Peter Howard now, I am sure he would agree with what I am about to say. Unfortunately, as you will see, he can no longer be communicated with. So I speak now for both of us.

We grow up, all of us, in an ocean of suggestions. There is a Zen story about two fishes arguing about the existence of the ocean. "It's all around you... you are surrounded by it...you've lived in the ocean all your life," the first fish claims. "Show me! Prove it... where is it?" says the second fish. What we call the "self" is a creation of the ocean of suggestions we live in, which is so all pervasive and obvious we cannot sense its existence.

On the one hand, I agree with fish number one, and profess a faith in something that I can't exactly see or touch or sense. On the other hand, I rebel, and refuse to believe in anything not empirically demonstrable. So, I am schizophrenic. I am crazy because I believe I have an adequate metaphysical reason for believing in only the physical plane (roses are red, violets are blue, I'm schizophrenic and so am I).

I've been trying to cure myself by taking a more sympathetic view of other people, some of them teachers, who (like fish number one) claim to have developed a "sixth sense" or a "greater awareness." Among them are those who say they can perceive God's sustenance flowing around us in a bright golden stream of sound and light, which, like gravity or oxygen, sustains us in a positive but ineffable way. I think that is probably a good way to look at life but that maybe we make too much of it, turning it into an idea that becomes sacred and removed from the experience of life; glorified as a concept. Then, the attempt at worshipping *Being* (out of gratitude) becomes worshipping *God* (as an idea, and out of obligation), which IS a kind of worshipping the devil, because the concept is just a concept and not God. That is a hell of a way to live. Nevertheless, both of my schizophrenic selves and all the rest of the teachers agree on one essential baseline principle: *our lives are being primarily determined by something we can't perceive with our senses.*

John Bleibtreu, author of *The Parable of the Beast,* talks about an insect which can't see, but which nevertheless pulls pine needles into its small burrow butt-end first. The insect has developed an exceptional sense of taste, so that it can distinguish between the butt-end and the spread-end of sets of pine needles. The insect can't see, but it can get along O.K. without sight. It could be that we have developed a similar viable alternative for getting along in the world though blinded by our minds. And our alternative way of getting along may be a more sophisticated method of orienting ourselves, but we just can't see it, being blinded by our concepts. It may be, as Peter Howard suggests, that a more intense grounding in gravity and sensation leads one to the tastier and better-oriented transcendent spiritual life based on the wisdom of insecurity. That may not make much sense to you yet, but stay tuned. Such theo-biological speculations are what this whole book is about. There may be a bolt of lightning that splits you in half, as it did Peter.

We so-called "mental health professionals" have undergone a lot of stress in recent years and are in need of some compassion from the general public. I have spent one lifetime already as a psychotherapist. I am beginning another as a writer. This book is about a rather enigmatic relationship between two psychotherapists. (Or should I say three psychotherapists, since one was schizophrenic?)

Those of us who are relatively awake have had to undergo radical changes in our ways of thinking in recent years. These changes have disoriented us and made us actually reverse what we thought about a number of things. For example, many of us now believe that there is no such thing as hypnotism. Or, more accurately, we no longer believe in non-hypnotism. Hypnotic suggestions are the order of the day. We find ourselves more or less adrift in a sea of suggestions. We have perhaps had a better opportunity to know about the ocean of suggestions than anyone else. We have talked to a lot of people about what is going on in their lives and we have tried out a lot of theories trying to help people learn how to not suffer so much. Freud used a lot of electrical treatments and massages for years, and then, concluding that they were not valid, invented a new machine of theory and a technique, which we now know works to about the same degree as the electrical treatments and massages did. The theories and techniques make one feel a little better for a while, and if you keep believing in them and repeating them they last a little longer, and then their effect is negligible. We all have our medicine shows, and one is just about as good as another if the practitioner is an artist at making suggestions.

What can we do then, with a sea of suggestions? Yogis and Buddhas of various kinds suggested one thing quite a long time ago. We just remain aware of the sea of suggestions through getting the suggestion that we all live in a sea of suggestions. What good will that do? I don't know. The suggestion that we live in a sea of suggestions may just make us more wary...maybe more paranoid. Because these big oceans of suggestions, called cultures, are dangerous. Cultures are oceans of suggestions made up of individuals who are themselves seas of suggestions.

Whole cultures learn to want to be hurt and suffer, and are accommodated by adjoining cultures who want, just as much, to strike back. We all want to avenge the wounds of our own earlier sufferings because all experience suggests that it helps to hurt back. Peter Howard, the person who is the primary focus of this book, has made a little rhyme about this dilemma:

"Romans and Jews,
Greeks and Turks,
French and Germans;
Whatever works.
Protestants and Catholics,
Iraqis and Kurds,
All mankind
Will kill for words."

All those oceans and minor seas of human beings in alliances and enmities that Toynbee describes in *A Study of History*, that we have all witnessed in our own lives during this last, most murderous of all centuries, are like the ebb and flow of a tide, that goes on and on in an unending cycle. Hermann Hesse wrote from that same transcendent perspective about the raging river of life within us individually and outside of us collectively. There are many more wise people in many more traditions whose conclusions are the same: *that we often live in our minds, in agreement with each other—but largely out of touch with reality.*

Introduction

Is there no real reality? These rocks and this sky and this hand I pinch myself with—are these not real? Maybe Fritz Perls, the father of Gestalt therapy, was right when he said sensations are the basis of knowing reality. But sensations and perceptions are suggestions too. They are of a different order, but still have that ephemeral passing quality all mere suggestions have. They die by the second, but they are simply the best suggestions we have for the moment. Visceral suggestions are more related to gravity and more trustworthy than the conceptual pool of the culture and the mind. The only pedagogical stance for a body-centered psychotherapist is that sensate suggestions, rather than social suggestions, are the best basis for integration of experience and choice of a direction for living life. There is certainly no reason to not kill yourself based on that.

Some of my friends who have raised children wouldn't let their kids go to the movies or watch TV unless they knew the content in advance. They have recognized and rightly feared the power of the myths that their children might dine on. Their attempts to control by limiting exposure failed, of course. The oceans own us more than we own them. The best we can do is get a boat.

People who hold the view of life that includes an awareness of an ocean of suggestions that ebbs and flows, are becoming more numerous now. It is almost inevitable that people get a perspective on what we are living in the middle of, simply because of how vastly we have expanded the ocean. The Internet, satellite TV, cell phones, hand-held computers and hundreds of other technological breakthroughs make it impossible for us to ignore the ongoing flood of suggestions. Our overwhelming ocean of speed media transport of suggestions has revealed itself. *We are beginning to see what we live in.*

Because of all this, I decided to edit this book. This book is about, and at the same time a part of, the ocean of suggestions and it tells the tale of a man who lived in a boat, from whom we all may be able to learn valuable lessons.

> *Brad Blanton*
> *Sparrowhawk Farm*
> *September 2004*

BOOK I

The Case of Peter X:
A Modern View of Paranoid Schizophrenia with Delusions of Grandeur

By

Victor Myerson, M.D.

(Condensed and edited by Dr. Brad Blanton)

tHIS IS A STORY of a man who had a psychotic break, and then, through treatment, recovered. I have written this story to clarify what a psychotic break is, and to exemplify the model of how one loses touch with reality. We shall call this man Peter X. During the time Peter was in need of hospitalization and treatment, he was in training with me to become certified as a psychoanalyst.

This story, I say, is about a model psychosis. The story begins with a particular therapy session in which I asked Peter X to play the role of his most frustrating patient. I often do this with training therapists whose first problems with patients usually have to do with over-identification, i.e., they can't always tell the difference between themselves and their patients. He experienced more difficulty than most trainees with this task. Later it came to light that his most difficult patient was this extraordinary second personality of his own.

My usual practice with trainees is to record all of their sessions so they can review them later if they wish. Slightly edited transcriptions of the tapes from these sessions are the basis for most of this account of the course of therapy. I have tried to remain non-prejudicial in my editing of the transcripts by adhering to two principal criteria: the reduction of the bulk of the material and necessary revisions to conceal the identity of the patient.

Peter's mind developed a "spirit-friend," who first started becoming a part of his confabulations when he began selecting out excerpts from therapy sessions of various patients he was seeing. He contended that a unitary spirit-personality was emerging spontaneously in a number of his patients at uncalled-for times, and with statements apparently unrelated to the psycho-dynamics of the patients involved. He also claimed that this was a specific and direct communication via these people to him, Dr. Peter X, requesting his help as a therapist. His delusion was that the spirit was seeking help from him by visiting in on the lives of these various patients. The delusion also grew to incorporate the idea that the exchange of therapeutic services was mutual—that both Peter and the "spirit" were actually doing psychotherapy with each other.

I must admit that though I was never "taken in" by Peter's psychosis, I was continually fascinated by his ability to lend validity to an absurd hypothesis.

Victor Myerson, M.D.

Philadelphia, September 1998

CHAPTER I

The Eternal Split-Second
Sound-Light Being

"J

UST AT THAT BREAKING POINT of first light, our little boat rounded the reefs and came peacefully across the mouth of the harbor. The light at the front of the boat was still on. The morning was at just that point of transition where the light was on solely as a beacon for others in the area, rather than our work. I had taken my usual break and stood watching carefully, with the boat silent, trying to demarcate increments of change so as not to be taken by surprise. But the slow turning of night to day had come again in an instant and despite all my careful attention, dawn shook the world without a sound. Reaching back to grasp it, I died again."

(Julia Hilton, 25th session, Friday morning, Oct. 6)

"I re-emerged and in the same man and place (which is rare) and for a few precious minutes more, glided on that small quiet boat into time again.

"Bird-sounds chattered and peeped and mixed with the new light, escorted us like a regal procession into the harbor. We actually giggled out loud with the birds and his good pipe and a big catch and the gray-blue ecstasy of first color. Then, he thought, this is just like... and I thought, I wish I could find a permanent body like this so... and we departed each other—him to the past and me to the future—and I died again."

(Mark Reynolds, 3rd session, in hospital, Friday afternoon, Oct. 6)

"I have become differentiated out of the ethereal mass-less-ness time and time again—in those instances where for a brief flash I have become one with a receptor-human, and together with him experienced being. But inevitably it's just a flash... then I return again from being into the hum...."

(Leon Marx, clinic, Tuesday, Oct. 11)

"I wish to hell I could find a permanent body. I never know where in the world I'm going to turn up. All I know is that I will be in some person whose receptor turns on, often at exactly dawn. (Long Pause) ... What a beautiful word, dawn.

"D A W N. It sounds just like what it is and yet can never quite be described. I said, "Exactly dawn," trying to be precise about the ineffable. But in crude words I must try to say the time... (Long pause).... Say the time. I must try to say the time ... because the information will be important to you as my therapist. But we'll get into that a little later."

(Neil Shift, Clinic, Thursday, Oct 20)

"Daybreak always comes before sunrise. Something happens before sunrise and at daybreak. A switch is thrown, some kind of connection is made, and a merger emerges. We can never catch just how, but at that non-specific time of dawn it most easily happens. Daybreak does the trick and sunrise gets the credit... dawn... sounds like y a w n...

"Anyway, it was when the big light appears just a little bit, that was for me the beginning of repetition of experience that helped me order my eternal life into some kind of meaningful identity. For I learned to live in the first light and pursue it around the face of the earth and learn by making that circle into a straight line just as humans do. And it was through this learning that it has become possible for me to identify with humans and get into my present fix and come to you for help."

(Don Speltzer, group session, clinic, Friday, Oct 21)

(Peter said of these last two quotes from his transcripts: "Notice that reference is made here to daybreak as in the previous statement. The patients involved have never met!")

"I knew I was becoming more human-like as I more often separated out... because more and more often I would catch myself, just before blinking out, wishing. For example, recently off Tierra del Fuego, I heard myself saying, 'I wish this would end quickly,' because it was cold and miserable where I had turned up in this poor drunk man's body who had fallen into the sea. I came to him in his flash of cold in the dawn light ... and he blinked out with me that day.

"I wished. And it's in the wishing—on my own and along with others—that I have learned of despair. What a wonder! ... That mental-physical-space-time-nexus-locus-unit-machine-of-flesh called human being. I have come to yearn for a body. I want to be one of you. I yearn for something that to you is a commonplace, everyday, taken-for-granted, not always perceived or felt, almost utterly unexamined thing—called life in the body. But at the same time, from hope, this great despair, I have come for the first time to love and understand the joy I have always had with nothing to measure it by. And I don't want to lose this precious ecstasy, or trade it in...disorganized and disoriented as it may be, unlocated to be sure, but nevertheless my present, and valued existence. So I roll like clouds in turmoil, desiring limitation and wanting no limits. But who am I? Or, should I say, 'Who is this?'— this discorporate corporation of instances—wishing. I have become more human, but I don't know if that is what I really wish. So I have learned through hope, to worry (and I don't really want to unlearn it), but I worry that I will lose all the precious benefits of my present life. Can you help me?"

(Norman Lee, outpatient clinic, 53rd session,
Wednesday, Oct.29.)

The foregoing excerpts, in writing, supposedly direct quotes from his patients, were presented to me by Dr. Peter X in the 46th training session, near the end of the first six months of his two-year post doctoral internship in psychotherapy under my supervision. Prior to this time, his work with patients, both in the hospital and in the outpatient clinic, had been exceptionally good.

When I say his work was exceptional, I feel I should inform the reader, in all modesty, that such a statement from me is not a frequent occurrence in this training hospital. But Peter was different in many ways. To begin with, he wasn't fresh out of graduate school or medical school as most of our interns are. He had spent six years "out in the world" after receiving his doctorate in psychology, had been in therapy and received earlier training, especially in Gestalt therapy, and had in fact been a practicing psychotherapist for a couple of years before entering our program. He came to us in pursuit of his own interest in doing work with a wider range of patients and further training in a medical facility with a more classical orientation. Although he seemed to have just the right combination of intuitive and intellectual skills to be an excellent psychotherapist, and he knew that I had a rather high opinion of him, we had had some pretty serious trouble in the two months preceding this session. His style of doing therapy was abrupt and somewhat charming, but he had a tendency to over-identify with his patients, to suffer more than is necessary on their behalf, and to make radical and sometimes erratic recommendations about actions they should take in the world. Some of these recommendations, some of his patients had acted on, and proceeded to get themselves, and in one case, the hospital, in a great deal more trouble than they had anticipated or were capable of handling. I had been forced to rein Peter in pretty hard. In some instances, he admitted having been in error and in some he disagreed with me. The result of both was that he worked harder and harder, on the one hand to keep my approval and on the other, to prove himself right, in spite of me.

Our last several sessions had been cool and businesslike, with many quiet spaces. I could tell that he was preoccupied with something and I had been waiting for him to pick a time to talk. This session had begun in a very guarded fashion as well, and the hour was almost over before he handed me the typewritten excerpts with some trepidation, and asked me to read them. By the time I had finished reading, his anxiety had apparently taken on a bit of a jovial mask.

"Well, Doctor, what do you think?" he said.

I responded predictably by reflecting his question back to him, and he, just as predictably, proceeded to answer himself.

"I think I'm doing therapy with a spirit."

For a while, not another word was spoken. He was looking at me carefully, trying to note any slight evidence of my reaction. I sat quietly. For a moment we were frozen there, careful observer observing careful observer. I was surprised by what he had said and by what he had given me, but I was also aware of the need for calmness and control and patience to see how the situation would turn out, with a minimum of participation on my part. If this was a joke, I could afford to be the butt of it. If this was, in fact, the beginning development of an authentic delusional system, then I was being looked at with that cuttingly wary perception of a paranoid and I'd best be on my toes. So I waited.

"He calls himself 'The Eternal Split-Second Sound Light Being.'"

I wondered, of course, how long this business had been going on. I knew better than to ask as well as I knew there was really no need to ask any more. The beginning revelation had been made, the dam was broken, and now all we had to do was wait a bit, and it would all come.

Peter smiled at me in his most seductive, winning way. I smiled back at him. Pleasant. Neutral. Controlled. He laughed. I continued to smile. Then he went on.

"These excerpts I just gave you came exactly as they are written, out of the mouths of the patients I've been working with, just when they had been surprised. Something they said, or something I said, surprised them. Either that, or they were in a hypnagogic state after the relaxation exercises we've been doing in groups."

Again he paused. I waited. He grimaced a little.

"Listen, I'm a bit anxious right now. But that's to be expected, isn't it? I'm very concerned about what you're thinking. I want you to believe me. You probably won't. You're thinking right now that I'm crazy. I may be, but please listen to me seriously, anyway."

"I'm listening."

"O.K., but I mean *really* listen..."

"O.K., *but*..." I said, pointing out to him that "but" was a way of negating the 'O.K.' and nudging him back to the point.

"All right, all right, goddammit, keep playing Doctor..." he said (impatient, but not really angry). "I'll go on. I have to go on..."

"I'm more than a little uptight, because, as you probably have guessed, I've been holding back for a long time."

Then he paused again. He was bent over in his chair, hands gripped together staring into the corner of the room, not so jovial any more. And I noticed, seeing him that way, how much I'd been missing of real evidence of fatigue. I think my expression did change a little because I really did feel sorry for him. He noticed the change immediately. Then, with a great effortful sigh, it came.

"Look, I think maybe I am going crazy. And if not, thinking about this craziness is driving me crazy. I mean, what's going on here is: I'm a therapist. O.K.? I'm a therapist. I am also in therapy and supervision with you. And what I have to work on now is a little problem I have of doing therapy with a spirit...I mean, that's pretty goddamned far out for openers!—And I just know you won't believe me either—but wait, that's not all. I hurt for this spirit...I feel sorry for it. I mean he has a hard row himself, wanting and not wanting to become human (talking very fast now). But he's becoming very human—I mean wanting two different things too much...he's obviously schizy and maybe I am too, and you may be too, for even listening to me at all (faster now) but he's schizy—he doesn't know whether he wants to be God or man—forever or now—and he's been having more and more of a problem with it. And yes, I know this whole thing could be, must be, some kind of fantastic crazy projection of my own, but it's my experience and all I have to go on and I'm tired of not telling you so I'm telling you!"

"Peter..."

"No! Let me finish! I could stand all of this (very fast now), but do you know what's really driving me crazy? (Laughter). What really gets me...I mean hurts! No, you don't know! Well, I'll tell you... I can't talk back to him! I mean, it's a fucking horror story..."

By now he had stood up and was pacing all over the room.

"I've got other evidence—I mean other excerpts—lots of other evidence—and this poor disembodied bastard is like one long scream in the universe—like bad but painful music—and I can't fucking talk back to him!"

He was nearly screaming himself.

"O.K., O.K., I hear you," I said. "I can hear you." I stood up, went over and took him by the arm and sat him down.

"Just take it easy for a minute." He was very tight all over. I let my hand stay on his shoulder. I was about to speak again when he started to cry. This surprised me too. He cried, almost grudgingly at first, shaking his head, but then he really began to sob. I stood there, touching him on the back of the neck and shoulders with my right hand, and rocking him a little. After a while, I saw and felt the tightness loosen and then loosen a little more, and flow with the tears. After a long time he started, very quietly, to talk again.

"Ah Jesus," he said. "Ah Jesus, I've been wanting to get into this a long time. I've been waiting a long time. I've been waiting a long time to tell you..."

Precisely then is when it all happened. Everything broke loose. I witnessed in action a clear psychotic episode, which left little doubt about a proper diagnosis, but which I must say, took me so much by surprise I was simply numb and did nothing to deal with it.

"*DID YOU HEAR THAT??!!*" He literally screamed at the top of his voice, leaping straight up out of the chair. He grabbed me by the shoulders. His face was three inches away. He shook me.

"Did you hear??! Did you hear it??! Did you hear it??!"

"No!" I said, literally in a panic myself. "No! Hear what??"

"HIM!" he said, "He talked!! He said I know you care about me—and I can hear you—you do talk back to me—I've been hearing you—THE SPIRIT!!" he yelled. "He said he could hear me!!" Then he began to jump all over the room. "Listen, he can hear...listen he can hear..." he chanted, almost singing, then stopping, turning his head sideways, listening, then moving on again.

What happened here, on reflection, and after the fact, is now quite clear to me. There had been a conversation—a sort of transformation through confusion in which my empathetic and accepting response to Peter was transported into what was now becoming his full-blown psychosis. And he attributed to his 'spirit' a response back, which was his way of incorporating an acceptance by me (which he had for some time feared would no longer be forthcoming) and which was too much for him to bear.

That seems clear enough now, but at the time I was still in quite a quandary. The session was nearly over and it was our last before the summer break. Peter was going to Greece for a well-deserved (and apparently much needed) vacation. My mind was going a mile a minute.

"Maybe the vacation will help," I was saying to myself. "Then again, the sudden relief might be even harder on him..." All the while, the therapist voice in my head kept saying, "Stop thinking and do something!"

"Peter, sit down!" I said, as firmly as I knew how, but louder than I had intended.

He sat down. Looked at me—wild-eyed but very attentive.

"We have about three minutes left in this session," I said, "and then you're leaving for Greece. I need some time to mull this over. You need some rest. I want you to take good care of yourself in Greece. Sleep, walk a lot, get as much rest and relaxation as you can. And, here, take this with you."

I had been writing while he was talking. I handed him the prescription along with a copy of a paperback book I had been using to write on. I don't know why I handed him the book with the prescription, but he took both of them anyway. Perhaps in my own confusion I hoped the book would distract him and shield or soften the impact of a prescription for Meccazine (a very strong tranquilizer). He took the paper and the paperback and just looked at me with a blank, and at the same time, elated expression on his face.

"O.K." he said. And he walked out.

I felt deeply dissatisfied. I felt shocked, unfinished, incomplete. Too many surprises. I wanted to call out to him...to say, "wait a minute—we need more time." But a psychiatrist, and particularly a training psychiatrist, and for good reason (namely, the very transference which precipitated this episode), can't do that. So I restrained myself, swallowing my dissatisfaction, and looked unconcerned, in case he might happen to glance back at me.

Just before the door closed, I saw the small round ball of the crumpled prescription fall to the floor and skitter under my secretary's desk.

CHAPTER 2

Case History

ITH THAT BRIEF INTRODUCTION to the case of Peter X, I will now give you some raw data about his background. It has become routine procedure in our training program now, that at the beginning of each post doctoral interns group (usually six people), every individual takes as much of a 2 hour session as he needs to tell the group the entire story of his life.

At the beginning of the second quarter of the Post Doctoral Internship Program, the interns are given typed transcriptions of their life stories and each intern is asked to respond briefly in writing to all of the stories, including his own. For their own story they were also instructed to "…free associate to the story of your life and think out loud about what kind of person your life has led you to become now—a sort of summary." This written self-summary is then used by all participants to diagnose and recommend treatment for each other.

Sociologically speaking, he comes from a working class family. He is the middle sibling in a family unit with 3.5 children (an older sister, younger brother and younger half-brother). He grew up in a rural area, made a transition to small-town life, and then suburbia, during adolescence, and then to city life in early adulthood. He moved from upper lower class, through lower middle class, to lower upper class. He was a problem child, then a conformist and a good boy, then a rebel, then a beatnik, then a civil rights activist, then an anti-war activist, and then a "hippie" and a member of the "counter culture." He was a Christian, Atheist, Agnostic, Socialist, Communist, Buddhist, Skeptic, in roughly that order. He was a laborer, academician, businessman, bureaucrat and self-employed person. There was something there for everyone.

Psychologically, he also did a number of double takes at critical stages of development. For example, here is an instance where the Oedipal conflict was not resolved in the usual way. At the critical age of not quite six years, he won. His father died and was replaced by him, the son, in the affections of the mother. Then defeat was snatched from the jaws of victory only a year later when his stepfather came on the scene. Then he still had the advantage of a male model to grow up with, but the relationship with that model was almost doomed to conflict from the beginning, regardless of what kind of a person the new father was. And the kind of person his stepfather was—alcoholic, violent, and abusive—caused Peter to have to grow up very fast in order to protect those he loved. So in a way, Peter had two Oedipal conflicts, both of which he won, given that he beat his step-father almost to death before leaving home at thirteen. Then, during adolescence, his identity was forged in a sequence of at least four separate social matrixes. He left the farm, at the age of thirteen and a half, and moved to a more hospitable and nurturant "family" with his brother-in-law and his sister, in a small college town. Then they moved to a larger city, and next, at the not so tender age of sixteen, he found himself on his own, in college.

What follows is Peter's written self-summary, just as it was presented to us. I wish to present the self-summary at this point prior to my own interpretation of his life story for several reasons. It provides more material for my analysis. It shows how his mind works. And it provides a clear indication of the direction his psychosis might take. Had I myself treated it more as a projective test or looked more carefully for warning signs about possible trouble, I might have been better prepared for what eventually happened.

Everything from here on is Peter's writing, and I tell you that now, so I can dispense with quotation marks. There is enough description of the parts of his life story that he is responding to as to not make it necessary to reprint the entire story. Although

I also want to add that he failed to respond to sections of his life story that for me also shed light on the nature of his psychosis —namely, those instances of conflict and unresolved feelings toward his father, his step-father, and various other male figures. I will say more of that later after you form your own impressions from Peter's associations to the content of his story. The italics in what follows are mine, and are done to exemplify what, for me, were hints at what eventually ensued.

CHAPTER 3
Associations to My Life Story

by Peter X

Y FIRST ASSOCIATION is to that Psilocybin-trip I took out in the country in Virginia, that I mentioned in my life story. That only happened a few years ago. When the drug first came on me I was pissing and whining back there in my psyche's corners about my daddy having died before I got through loving him and fighting with him and me never finding anybody else big enough to substitute for what a daddy is to a five year old. I came up seated at the foot of a gray stump bigger than a mountain. God said, "O.K., boy, you can break your back on me and I won't even remember your name." Actually, He didn't say that, He just implied it, but the message was quite clear. I can't tell you how obvious it was, how teensy-little-queechy-tiny-mere-pinsized-fartwelder-piss-ant I was sitting there at the foot of God—like an ant at the foot of Mount Kilamanjaro. And it was touch and go there for a while, but it was clear He didn't care much, one way or the other. Period.

Then the devil was there and he said, "Come on with me, man, you know what it's like." And the floods of memories of great pleasures came on me. I said, "Yeah, I know man, but why waste all those years of conditioning and learning and yearning to be a good man? Might as well let it work out"…not eager but kind of resigned. And the voice of the devil said, "God damn, God! You always take the ones I really want." Then God said to me, "Don't speak for twenty-seven days." He was talking to me. A deep voice right inside my head—"Don't speak for twenty-seven days." Just that. So I didn't. And some of my life's meaning got clearer in my head while my mouth was shut. Before that time in my life I had always thought that if I didn't keep talking and constantly take care of everybody, everything would fall apart. If I didn't keep talking and keep everything together and take care of everybody, things would go out of control. It turns out I was right. My whole life did fall apart. My wife left me. My community dispersed. And at the end of the twenty-seven days I was alone on a farm in Ohio with nobody to talk to. It's one of the best things that ever happened to me.

Now I'll tell you who I think I am. I am a member of an elite class of people who are undergoing a transition to power. I get

stoned two or three times a week and watch TV. I work occasionally. I profess not to value money, thereby exhibiting my valuing
of money. I have been stylishly radical for many years. I am on
the avant garde cutting edge of the moderately well socialized
pre-take-over generation. I am extremely pretentious (as this
statement reveals). I don't believe in elections anymore. I have
become stylishly embittered about the democratic process. I take
as much from the government as possible. I am idealistic to the
very edge of arrest. I am divorced after ten fairly happy years of
marriage. I have tried "community" a bit. I have fucked around
a lot lately. The last several years I changed jobs or changed
places within a job fairly often—like once every year or year and
a half. I act sincere and I don't believe in sincerity. I have stayed
consistently three years in front of what's on TV, particularly the
news. I made it in Academia and I like to play like it didn't
count. Most of it, I truly believe, didn't. I don't believe in truly
believing. I am extremely critical. I am an incurable idealist. I
act on many of my fantasies—more than normal; or at least I like
to believe that, and that, too, I think, is typical. I think I may
be angrier than most people, but anger, too, is typical really of
most of us these days. All in all, I think I'm a lucky man. I hardly ever say that out loud. I don't mean to be too happy. I don't
want to praise the system any. I am a typical middle class neurotic. My life may best serve only as a warning to others.

Illusions are our only hope. Hope is the source of despair.
We all have learned to hope and that is where depression comes
from. It comes, I think, from all of us going to too many movies

after hearing lots of radio programs. For me it was radio for years, television for years, and then the ongoing media explosion ever since. So I live a lot in fantasy, more than humans ever have before, as all of us who are alive now do. We should study me. We should watch me carefully. I am "exhibit A" for the defense. What is being defended is civilization. The case is lost but the testimony goes on.

By now you probably think I'm crazy, don't you? No, I'm not crazy and I'm not stupid. I'm not as fucked up as most of this may sound. I've just been taking some time out to be honest. I can fake my behavior and what I say, the way we are all supposed to, any time. My facade is a very good one. I am well protected. I am in the upper 2½% of the world's population with regard to intelligence. I scored in the ninety-ninth percentile on the *Watson-Glaser Test of Critical Thinking Ability*. My Ph.D. dissertation was entitled "Interrelated Aspects of Cognitive Organization of the Social World, Self Perception and Overall Mental Health." I have tangible proof of my alienation. I'm a professional. I'm a Gestalt therapist. I have been a businessman. I've taught in a university. I have all the power of rational, orderly, logical thought. I even know that you're not supposed to say rational and logical in the same sentence.

One of the reasons I am in this postdoctoral program is to deepen my perspective on the social context in which we all are living. I'm not much interested in just a clinical view any more. It doesn't help much. My field of specialization as a scholar was cognition. I know whole theories of thinking. But I'm still lost.

Baba Ram Dass wrote a book called, *Be Here Now*. In that book, Ram Dass said, his teacher in India (who's dead now) used to eat a lot of food as a way of "taking on Karma" from the person who gave it to him. I wonder how many people's Karma gets taken into me from a beer and a cheeseburger? No wonder I'm confused. Then again, think of all those freaks that handle health foods. The only way to find out where you're at is to notice what you feed yourself and notice what happens afterward. The ideas we feed on are about the same as the food—and they've already been handled by as many people. Here I am, desperate for meaning in my life, taking on ideas, like that idea of taking on Karma through what we eat, and playing with them.

Let me try again. I believed in God once at a very young age. Later on I learned that the higher power is in me. John Lennon said, "I believe in me." I believe that too, but have difficulty with the object of faith. Each of us is his own answer. I am my own answer. But my life story is just a tale about how I got twisted into a question.

So what am I like? Well, I think a lot. I think about death a lot. And what I think about death is this. Death is a part of the illusion of time. Plants don't worry about dying or particularly enjoy growing; they just grow. Knowing about death and time gives us a chance to enjoy ourselves and suffer. Lucky us. My friend Jordan says, "Death is a definition." Deaths are indeed definitions—all of them. And this is one, and this is one, and divorce and growing old and dispensing with your life story up to now, etc. I've died a lot and I think it's just a matter of God defining himself. We are here because God is so neurotic. He can't be sure of his own existence without a mirror. He is having a perennial identity crisis.

Yes, that's true for me all right. God is his own answer. Says "yes" to Himself to beat the Devil. Luckily for us the Devil exists, aren't we? It's all done with mirrors. I'm all done with mirrors. The ringing silence of true synthesis when we are one with ourselves strikes at the point of death, perhaps, because then we live in the space between the mirrors.

Hermann Hesse said this about death when one of his characters named Klein (which means *little*) drowned himself in a river...

> ...*In the gray darkness of the rain above the nocturnal lake the drowning man saw the drama of the world mirrored and represented: suns and stars rolled up, rolled down; choirs of men and animals, spirits and angels, stood facing one another, sang, fell silent, shouted; processions of living beings marched towards one another, each mis-understanding himself, hating himself, and hating and persecuting himself in every other being. All of them yearned for death, for peace; their goal was God, was the return to God and remaining in God. This goal created dread, for it was an error. There was no remaining in God. There was no peace. There was only the eternal, eternal, glorious, holy being exhaled and inhaled, assuming form and being dissolved, birth and death, exodus and return, without pause, without end. And therefore there*

was only one art, only one teaching, only one secret: to let yourself fall, not to resist God's will, to cling to nothing, neither to good nor to evil. Then you were redeemed, then you were free of suffering, free of dread—only then. His life lay before him like a landscape with woods, valleys, and villages that could be viewed from the ridge of a high mountain range. Everything had been good, simple and good, and everything had been converted by his dread, by his resisting, to torment and complexity, to horrible knots and convulsions of wretchedness and grief. There was no woman you could not live without and there was no woman with whom you could have lived. There was not a thing in the world that was not just as beautiful, just as desirable, just as joyous as its opposite. It was blissful to live, it was blissful to die, as soon as you hung suspended along in space. Peace from without did not exist; there was no peace in the graveyard, no peace in God. No magic ever interrupted the eternal chain of births, the endless succession of God's breaths. But there was another kind of peace, to be found within your own self. Its name was: Let yourself fall! Do not fight back! Die gladly! Live gladly! All the figures of his life were with him, all the faces of his love, all the guises of his suffering. His wife was pure and as guiltless as himself. Teresina smiled childishly. A murderer, whose shadow had fallen so heavily across Klein's life, smiled earnestly into his face, and his smile said that his act, too had been one way to redemption; it too had been breath, it too a symbol, and that even killing and blood and atrocities were not things that truly existed, but only assessments of own self-tormenting souls...A hundred times, full of dread, he had attended his own death, had seen himself dying on the scaffold, had felt the razor blade cutting into his own throat and the bullet in his own temple—and now that he was dying the death he had feared, it was so easy, so simple, was joy and triumph. Nothing in the world need be feared, nothing was terrible—only in our delusions do we create all this fear, all this suffering for ourselves, only in our own frightened souls do good and evil, worth and worthlessness, craving and fear arise...Water flowed into his mouth and he drank. From all sides, through all his senses, water flowed in; everything dissolved in it. He was being drawn, breathed in. Beside him, pressed against him, as close together as the drops of water, floated other people; Teresina floated, the old comedian floated, his wife, his father, his mother and sister, and thousands, thousands, thousands of others, and pictures and buildings as well, Titian's Venus and Strasbourg Cathedral, everything floated, pressed close together, in a tremendous stream, driven by necessity, faster and faster, rushing madly—and this tremendous, gigantic, raging stream of forms was racing towards another stream just as vast, racing just as fast, a stream of faces, legs, bellies, animals, flowers thoughts, murders, suicides, written books, wept tears, dense, dense, full, full, children's eyes and black curls and fish-heads, a woman with a long rigid knife in her bloody belly, a young man resembling himself at the age of twenty, that vanished Klein of the past. How good that this insight too was coming to him now: now that there was no time! The only thing that stood between old age and youth, between Babylon and Berlin, between good and evil, giving and taking, the only thing that filled the world with differences, opinions, suffering, conflict, war, was the human mind, the young, tempestuous, and cruel human mind in the stage of rash youth, till far from knowledge, still far from God. That mind invented contradictions, invented names; it called some things beautiful, some ugly, some good, some bad. One part of life was called love, another murder. How young, foolish, comical this mind was. One of its inventions was time. A subtle invention, a refined instrument for torturing the self even more keenly and making the world multiplex and difficult. For them man was separated from all he craved only by time, by time alone, this crazy invention! It was one of the props, one of the crutches that you had to let go, that one above all, if you wanted to be free, The universal stream of forms flowed on, the forms inhaled by God and the other, the contrary forms that he breathed out. Klein saw those who opposed the current, who reared up in fearful convulsions and created horrible tortures for themselves: heroes, criminals, madmen, thinkers, lovers, reli-

gions. He saw others like himself being carried along swiftly and easily, in the deep voluptuousness of yielding, of
consent. Blessed like himself. Out of the song of the
blessed and out of the endless cries of torment from the
unblessed there rose over both universal streams a trans-
parent sphere or dome of sound, a cathedral of music. In
its midst sat God, a bright star, invisible from sheer brightness, the quintessence of light, with the music of the universal choirs roaring around in eternal surges. Heroes and
thinkers emerged from the universal stream, prophets.
"Behold, this is the God the Lord and his way leads to
peace," one of them cried, and many followed him.
Another proclaimed that God's path led to struggle and
war. One called him light, one night, one father, mother.
One praised him as tranquility, one as movement, as fire,
as coal, as judge, as comforter, as creator, as destroyer, as
forgiver, as avenger. God himself did not call himself anything. He wanted to be called, wanted to be loved, wanted to be praised, cursed, hated, worshipped, for the music
of the universal choirs was his temple and was his life—
but he did not care what names were used to hail him,
whether he was loved or hated, whether men sought rest
and sleep or dance and furor in him. Everyone could seek.
Everyone could find. Now Klein heard his own voice. He
was singing. With a new, mighty, high reverberating voice
he sang loudly, loudly and resoundingly sang God's praise.
He sang as he floated along in the rushing stream in the

midst of the millions of creatures. He had become a prophet and proclaimed. Loudly, his song resounded; the vault of music rose high; radiantly, God sat within it. The stream roared tremendously along.

What a vision Hesse had his man Klein have as he died! I get it! I am moved by it! I understand it! And I know there is a vision of the great truth in it, and out of my whole life and many dyings and fears of death and useless struggle I can hear him! And I hear Klein as he sings praise to all the manifestations of life and calls them God. Once when I was on LSD, the whole world was trembling and my eyeballs were trembling and my whole body was trembling. The trembling itself became the stream of life. I was filled with joy and awe at the magnificence of all of trembling being. But I don't only get this picture just from acid and from Herman Hesse, I get this picture when I read a book called *Red Giants and White Dwarfs*, that the universe, that all of astronomy, and all of sub-atomic physics fit together in a pattern and one of the central, basic elements of that pattern is a kind of attraction, a borderline careful thing where Yes and No are never clear enough to win, where trembling is the theme, where like two magnets, a careful balance is held and energy maintains its speed in the form of matter. I want to be a similar appreciator and magician for social reality—to see and love and praise the brilliance of human beings for their mutual care and co-intelligence and tragic mistakes and sing their praises. What I would like to be is the most compassionate man who ever lived. My mental image of compassion used to be looking down at people, animals and all living things. Now I think compassion is much more than that. Looking down at things from a transcendent position is only knowledge, which usually just leads to categorization and abuse. Wisdom has to do a parallel view of all of the energy of the universe, while looking out on it, without putting it down.

Soren Kierkegaard was a Danish theologian and psychologist who wrote beautifully and exactly about the nature of man and God. He said that Jesus said something like, "There is a possibility that you could love your neighbor, love yourself and love your life, whatever it brings you." I think that to love life is to love tension. If we are really going to love our lives, we have to learn to love the dynamic tension between opposite tendencies, events, ideas—the hypocrisy of being. Variable and inconsistent dynamic tension—tension which does not remain the same so that we can get used to it—tension that sways, develops, falls, subsides, increases, tightens, disappears. The tension between doing yoga and smoking dope, between quitting cigarettes and eating more and getting fat, between intellectual pretentiousness and earthy crudity, between fucking and thinking. All of life as it is experienced, is a series of tensions—which vary. Eyeball variable tensions are called sight; skin variable tensions are called touch; variables inside nose, mouth, throat and tongue tensions are called taste and smell; variable bodily tensions in response to internal thought and emotional attachment are called stress. "May I have your tension please?" "Now pay tension, kiddies. First we have to work on our tension span—try to get a longer tension span." To love life is to love tension. Hindus and Buddhists say tension is suffering—go beyond to bliss. Even some Christians say affirm tension but don't be trapped by it. Love your way beyond it.

But the problem in that is, I don't really know much about love. When I am feeling lonely or desperate I care for whoever is around very much. Or, if no one is around, I care very much for some people. I fantasize about people that I was once related to and miss them. At other times, when I'm not feeling desperate or lonely, I don't care so much. There is a relationship between how needful I feel, and my protestations of love for another— probably also between how needful I feel, and protestations of love for myself. I don't trust myself with regard to what I mean by love and I don't think anyone else should either. "God loves those who love themselves," is true. I'll tell you something else that's true. God hates those who love themselves. Both of those statements are lies. God doesn't speak much in English, but if He did He would say, "I am love and hate. I am up and down. I'm high and I'm normal. I'm transcendental and I'm earthy. I have light and darkness to dispense. I give you your freedom to choose what I have to offer and you may change your mind as often as you like, for my essence is ongoing life and ongoing per- mission to live in as many ways as life can come up with." As Job says in the play about him by Arthur Miller, "If God is good He is not God. If God is God he is not good. Take the even, take the odd. I would change it if I could." Our ability to transcend the dualities about God created by our minds, and to love all of being, takes a lot of heart,

Now I Know What I Want to Do with My Life

My primary objective is to go on beyond normal. The definition of "mental health" and the definition of "art" are the same. Perception plus conception is the source of creating art. Misconception plus perception is the source of creating shit. If artful noticing and living has a product others can experience, that product is called art. Whether the way one lives results in an esthetic product or not, the process of bringing about that unity of percept and concept such that one has an enhanced experience of being is itself art. I think that the openness and transcendent perspective of Herman Hesse and his man Klein, and Kierkegaard, and Arthur Miller, and thousands of others like them is living life as an artist, and that is what I want to do.

All of us love art. That's why people watch TV so much— Sunday football games, amateur hour, golf matches, etc. When we watch someone playing in a golf tournament we are fascinated when he or she conceptualize what they are going to do at each hole, look at where the ball landed from the last shot, figure out how to hit it, hit it, and get it into that hole with as few strokes as possible. When someone does this better than anybody else, they get awarded a prize at the end—a lot of money. That unity of perception, conception and action is artfully done and we support it the best we can, given how alienated most of us are from our experience as a result of our schooling, we still admire it when someone integrates their experience and their mind.

R.D. Laing says, and I agree, that behaving is a function of experience, and both behavior and experience are always in relation to someone or something other than self. That is, whatever the self is, it is something that responds to experience with behavior. Soren Kierkegaard said over three hundred years ago, "A being who relates to another being and relates also to that relationship, relates thereby to God." I think what he means is that a being who acknowledges the being of another human being, acknowledges thereby all of being. Other theologians, (Paul Tillich, for example) have the same idea for on-beyond-normal living—that through conscious relating each person could live his life as an art form.

The materials with which I work in the creation of my existence are the materials that I use like clay, as an artist, to create a life that is a work of art. Creating things in the material world that are the result of "getting it all together", and acting on it, is the art of living. In doing therapy with people I think our job is to turn them on to themselves as artists—to turn them on to the possibility of being great in the manifestation of their own uniqueness, i.e., the integration of their unique experience with their mind's ability to participate in creation.

Finally, the highest art for me is the art of compassion. And the people I particularly like working with, end up usually in one way or another, conducting therapy or the running of groups of some kind, as a way of beginning to develop their own art of compassion—because groups offer opportunities to experience separateness and discover relatedness. I continue to do therapeutic work primarily because of what I'm learning about how to be compassionate without looking down. When I work with people my best strength is my authentic curiosity. I say something like, "What do you feel in your body, and what do you imagine in your head, and how have you been getting them together lately, and how are you getting it together now, and what is your newest creation?" I didn't learn this from any training program or any school, but from living among us. A lot of what I've learned that I use in doing therapy came from taking L.S.D trips rather than from professional training. L.S.D. trips helped me to learn that there are cognitive trips, and there are perceiving trips, and there are acting trips, and they can be separate or together, and that none of them are a no-no—that the only no-no is getting trapped in one trip. Cognitive creations, for example (like this one) have a life of their own. I like writing this and I will probably like reading it over again once it's written, but I would hate like hell to be trapped at this particular place in my head, and not be able to get out of it. I really love to be turned on to food and sex and sensuality when I'm high on grass, but I wouldn't want it all the time. I like being in touch with people *but would hate having my in-touch-ness unalterably turned on, because I might accidentally watch the evening news for ten minutes in that state of mind, and go crazy.* But I must now confess that my life has led me to just such a trap. My in-touch-ness has been turned on and I don't like it when sometimes I can't turn it off and I'm having trouble with that.

Abe Maslow said we humans have a hierarchy of needs. Our primary needs are biological: eating, drinking and fucking. Before these needs are taken care of, any person who has them works for their fulfillment and uses his life energy for the task.

Once we become secure about fulfillment of biological needs and used to getting enough food, drink, shelter and sex, then we concern ourselves with social needs: we worry about acceptance from others. Our dreams and efforts turn from food and sex to dining with important people; having sex with celebrities; being looked up to and listened to by others; being respected—feeling successful and of a higher class than mere food grovelers.

After some period of time, sometimes a whole generation, acclaim gets boring, being successful becomes familiar, and keeping up the good image gets to be a drag, and not worth the effort anymore. After biological and social needs have been ful- filled, after we've been gratified and accepted enough, comes the more elite hell of striving for meaning, wanting to figure it all out. We are full and accepted and now we want life to have meaning. This is where we ask, "What's it all about, Alfie?" And this is where, for me, it all stops. We lose. The only meaning in life comes from our own compulsions to make it mean some- thing! For a long time I have been able to view the emptiness of no meaning, and fought hard and valiantly to go back to the bliss of earlier ignorance, but to no avail.

I know that this is not only my story. This is the story of what occurs to many, many people. This is also the story of Walter Mitty and Jack Armstrong and Amelia Earhart and Barry

Goldwater and Richard Nixon and Bill Clinton and the whole rags to riches to rags fable. Like a bad movie, we all move from self-glorification and intellectual pretentiousness, to success, to failure, to self-vilification and confession of weakness, and then do it all over again. I wonder if there was ever a way I could have stayed dumb and happy down on the farm if my daddy had lived?

Right now, Bob Dylan sings in the back of my mind about a lady he knew:

> *"Some speak of the future.*
> *My love, she speaks softly,*
> *She knows there's no success like failure,*
> *And that failure's no success at all."*

The truth is I'm afraid. I'm afraid of being too sensitive and going crazy. I'm afraid of everything I've talked about here, and everything I told about in my life story. I'm afraid of death. I'm afraid of love. The truth is, I'm not so wise as I pretend. The truth is that I've spent so much time in my life preparing for life; I can't stop preparing and start living.

Getting raised, hurt, entertained and educated, and finding out and knowing about life, is a bum path. We should stop "educating" and pushing children to learn, and try to keep each other dumb and happy. A lot of us know this. The other life stories in this group of interns confirm it. This is how we live, all of us. This. Keeping busy or getting high or drunk or distracted most of the time. We get born, spend a lot of energy preparing, get in the middle, and discover we don't have the energy to work to succeed anymore, and we don't know how to live without preparing and imagining and hoping for what is to come. Without working to succeed, what is there?

My despair doesn't come from being a social misfit. It comes from success. The things that were to come came. And then again. And again. Several times. And now anticipation itself is getting boring, knowing that you must live without hope and not being able to, and feeling bad about not being able to hope completely anymore, ever again.

If I found out I was dying of a terminal disease (as I've often imagined), I would be very sad. At the same time, I think often of killing myself. I think I want to die, and I want to know I'm going to, so I can be sad about it. Maybe I still want to feel sorry for myself. No, I don't want to, but aren't we all sad? Isn't it too bad about us? Yes, I do feel sorry for myself, because really I'm a pathetically sad, tragic case. Illusions are our only hope, and hope our only illusion. And I'm getting so tired.

CHAPTER 4
Theoretical Perspective on Peter's Lifestory and Self-summary

ETER SAYS HE IS TYPICAL of Americans in his age group. In the face of his unusual perspective on his life story, that seems at first glance to be a rather careless assertion. But when we look closer, what makes him unusual is that he has been through more of the typical conflicts and transitions of growing up in our culture than most of us have had to experience individually. So, I must say I agree with him (although we all know in this profession there is really no such thing as a "typical" case.) But this is one good reason for choosing him as an *exemplary* case.

I don't intend to do a complete case-history analysis at this point, but I do wish to make clear two critical judgments that are central to my interpretation of this case. First: after the age of six, Peter was forced to rely primarily on himself, and secondarily on the social matrix in which he lived. Second, as he developed competence in dealing with the diverse tasks one has to master in later childhood and adolescence, and forged his identity, he never completely trusted anyone again.

He developed his personality around something missing, around a hole in his being; namely, the nurturing and sustaining power of a close-knit family, which he could remember only vaguely, as something associated with an earlier time when his father was alive. In a way, this happens to all of us, but not as graphically. It will soon become clear what pertinence this has to the further development of the case.

CHAPTER 5

Return from Greece

PROBABLY AS AN ATTEMPT to please me, as well as to integrate his increasingly bizarre experience, Peter spent his three weeks in Greece not only reading, but writing a review of *Parable of the Beast*, the book by John Bleibtreu, which I had accidentally handed him with the prescription. I read the review and it was a good, thorough job. It got me interested enough to read the book. When I made a comparison between the review he had written and the book itself, it became clear to me that Peter was using the book to elaborate his psychosis. I mention this here only because reading that book may help if you have trouble with some of the following excerpts from Peter's first session with me after his return from Greece...

"Well, Doc, you're not as dumb as you look!"

Those were the first words out of Peter's mouth when he barged into my office after his trip. He was tanned and exuberant and the very picture of health, except for some evidence of strain around the eyes. His secretary had made his new appointment with my secretary. I knew he was coming, but we hadn't talked since his return four days earlier. Needless to say, I had spent some time worrying and wondering about what to do about Peter. After all, he was not only a patient, but also a training therapist, and I felt my responsibility went beyond just concern for him.

"You cagey bastard, giving me that book! We are the two greatest therapists I know of." And he actually slapped me on the back before he sat down. He stood up again almost immediately.

"We both know a secret about how we are sustained in being, and I didn't know we knew!" He laughed.

I didn't know what he was talking about.

"I had no idea you knew so much—and I had even less of an idea of how much I know," and he laughed some more.

"It's so simple..."

"Well, would you mind complicating it a little bit, so I can understand?" I said.

"O-ho! A hostile shrink trying to dampen my spirits! O.K., I will explain—and by the way, I don't blame you for being hostile toward me, and I'll get to that—but for now we'll just roll right on, and we'll deal with your problems later, ha, ha! What I have to say is, I know and you know, although you may not know you know, that we are both sustained in being by a lot of things, including gravity, atmospheric pressure, oxygen, and internal chemistry, but last and not least—and of great importance to me, and you—we are sustained by an impersonal transmitter. It's a light that hums. I'm also a light that hums sometimes, as are you. But this transmitter is quite impersonal. It happens all the time. Being aware of this transmitter is a personal (though rare) experience. The receiver has only personal experiences of the transmissions to go by (and most of the time is unaware of his experience of being sustained). 'Father' was Jesus' name for the sustaining rhythm, which is personally experienced. Awareness of being sustained is a deeply personal experience, for which one is (and Jesus was, and I am) grateful, but for which one does not owe gratitude—because the transmitter doesn't care: the transmitter is impersonal. The experience of being sustained by the rhythm is like being back in the womb, protected and provided for free of charge, and wholly given over to being wholly given over to.

"So, Jesus called it 'Father,' because it did a good job of taking care of him. The old Jews had said the transmitter was a hard ass. But Jesus said it was all goodness and light, because it descended on him like a dove, and gave him a hard life, but a flattering role. So he called the transmitter 'Father,' although I don't want to do that now myself, because then we get the

Baptist Church, and other perversions having to do with Jesus not having been too politically astute, right from the very beginning. But the old Jews and Jesus and me all agree on one thing—it's always there. 'Perfect Father' is not really a bad name, because it does sustain you with being... fed Jesus well, and gave him enough nails to hang himself, so to speak. Anyway, 'Father' was Jesus' name for the sustaining rhythm, which is personally experienced. Charan Singh, who is alive and well in India this very day, calls it the audible light. I, as a receiver of the transmission (and you as well, I might add), am a historical memory/eternal now synthesis/perceiver. That's what I am, by God (so to speak), as well as you; maybe coordinated via the pituitary gland. Which is to say, the receiver of audible light rhythm transmissions is a personally experiencing, historical memory/eternal now synthetic perceiver, whose receptions of various tunings-in on the light are coordinated via the pituitary gland and the limbic brain. So we come to know God, like Rodin discovers beautiful faces and bodies emerging out of marble. Now, is that complicated enough? Do you understand me?"

Without waiting for an answer he said, "What surprises me is that you must have known all this and not told me. How come?" He had been speaking incredibly fast.

Again, despite all my thought beforehand, I didn't really know what to do. He was putting on quite a show. And he was laughing a lot, although, in a way, it was more like a very heightened, general affective state, as though he might cry as fluidly as he had been laughing. So I said, a little sarcastically, "Well, I didn't tell you everything, because I didn't think you were quite ready yet." He ignored the sarcasm, or missed it completely, took what I said literally, and charged on.

"Ha! Just as I suspected! But now, let me tell you something, you may not know you know. I've learned something of the mechanics of how God loves us, and I'll lay it on you for free. You see..."

For the first time he took a seat in the chair opposite me. I should have stopped him here, but I was fascinated, so I let him go on. I was reminded for a moment of Robert Lindner's patient who was a physicist (in *The Fifty Minute Hour*) who built an entire world order on another planet using science as a tool for his psychosis. Lindner was so fascinated with the story he couldn't bear interrupting his patient to get him out of his delusional system. I thought to myself, "Well, now, you've been getting older and worrying a lot and don't often get well entertained ... and he is crazy, but at least he got back from Greece, and we've got time to let him sing a while..."

So he sang some more. This is almost verbatim from the tape from here on out. The words are all there; the gestures and the actions, unfortunately, were not recorded. Let your imagination fill in the blanks like Peter said he used to do with radio shows in the past.

"You see, like when you take acid or mushrooms and experience synesthesia—like *seeing* music and *hearing* pictures—it seems perfectly natural to say 'that smells brown' or 'she sounds warm.' When you say those things they make sense, although the words are not adequate and sound funny. But you know that brown-ness and its smell and the sound of warm are inseparable. So when we think about these experiences with words, we are fragmenting ourselves. It's not that we do anything to synthesize sense information when we're high, it's that we *stop doing*— i.e., stop fragmenting and attend to our original home base unitary experience. Well, that's the rhythm—the old cosmoroo—the white light in the night—what it was I was talking about! The light that hums. It's the good old pineal gland maybe, the third eye, that we hear it with—the light I mean."

"Anyway, seeing music has something to do with a cellular experience in the brain which accepts all the separate senses' information as telling the same story. The same movie of the outside world recorded on five-channel stereo for your listening (tasting, touching, seeing, smelling) pleasure. One cell says to the other, 'Well, it's all the same to me, man.' And so it is. But, I digress. The question is, can we tune in (by tuning in to our own cells, or as I have come to call me—our own cellfs) and transmit back to the rhythm? And the answer is, of course, '*of course!*' That's why faith healing works. But the other question is how, and I don't know the answer to that yet, so I want a little more therapy."

Finally there was a pause. He looked at me. I said, "What happened to you in Greece?"

"Ah, I woke up at 4:00 A.M. every day and I've been talking to the spirit directly and to John Bleibtreu ever since the moment you put me in touch with them. That's how I learned what I just told you about my own 'cellf.' I introduced my spirit to John Bleibtreu and they said, in me, 'Every cell a self and every self a cell and a chicken in every pot and pot in every chicken and a garage in every Volkswagen, and a woman in every port and a port in every woman!" A port in every woman! Ha! Ha! [He came over and nudged me in the ribs with his elbow.] Dig it! Freudy!

"Greece was wonderful. Everything smelled of blue gold light and the spirit of the lord descended upon me like a dove via my own ACTH system. I had a wonderful time and I wish you had been there. I became more cellf- conscious and less embarrassed and I want to thank you from the bottom of my pineal gland for everything—except the Meccazine, which, of course, I didn't take. And as sure as there is a Great White Whale who lives on forever, you'll get a fine reward in heaven herself."

"Did you sleep?"

"Not much. I was too busy talkin' to my 'cellf.'"

"And have you been this 'speedy' all of the time?"

"Yes, and I took acid. And I stayed up forty two hours walking, once."

We sat and looked at each other. I took a drink of water from the water glass beside me. He drank some water too. We looked at each other.

I said, "Well, Peter, I want you to check into the hospital."

(Pause)

"You're kidding."

"I'm quite serious. You are relieved of your own hospital duties as of now, and for an indefinite period. I'd like you to commit yourself voluntarily this evening. I will come and see you there tomorrow."

(A long pause)

"I can't believe you, man! Why? You want me to go into the hospital? Are you trying to drive me crazy? I mean, just because I've been so happy about what you've done for me and now..."

I said, "You are very elated. But, if you're paying such careful attention to your 'cellf' then let yourself notice the strain that is obvious to me. You are still tired. You're exhausted. And you are still speeding. And you are going to have to take some medication and rest and work with me for a while. I am not punishing you. I am, however, seriously concerned about you. I'm glad about what has been happening with you in therapy with me, and I'm glad you've trusted me so far, and I think you should continue to do so, by entering the hospital."

When I stopped speaking he was looking directly at me in his former controlled way. The levity had disappeared from his features as well as his voice. I had made my statement and he had heard. Then, he made his statement.

"I'm interested in one thing. That is: how to get in touch with—and as much as possible stay in touch with—that which is outside me and connected to every inside of me and sustains me. You and my spirit-friend have both been teaching me well. But, I don't want that connection with him interfered with. That kind of help I don't want. And, if I'm forced to choose between him and you, you lose. And don't you forget it."

He looked me right in the eye as he said these words and he

was elegant. He had acceded to my demand, maintained his own integrity, asked for help, given me a warning, expressed appreciation and given a clue critical to an adequate diagnosis of his case—all in that one statement.

"I hear you," I said.

"O.K.," he said, "I'll be in the hospital at 7:00 p.m. tonight." He walked out.

The rationale for my decision to request that Peter commit himself to the hospital immediately was as follows: In addition to the generally heightened affective state, I noticed several things: (1) Peter was mildly, but constantly defying me; (2) he had begun calling his former "client" his friend; (3) his whole way of relating to me was more informal than we had ever been; (4) he pitted me against his "friend," in competition for his own allegiance; and (5) statements such as "...Jesus called it 'Father'...although I don't want to do that myself..." and stress on the words 'personal' and 'impersonal" had to do with his central problem in relationship to me.

I think he was trying hard to express appreciation to me, and even affection for me, but keep his distance. This was a re-enactment on an emotional level of his intense conflict with his stepfather when he was 7 or 8 years old. He had a need for a father and he needed equally as strongly to not show his need. His stubbornness in the face of adversity caused mainly by his stepfather, was the only way he had of maintaining his integrity as a person at so young an age. The re-emergence of this conflict at this point in Peter's life was a crisis, which was brought about by his having taken on the full-time load of a therapist, and by his attempt to control his conflict with me. It was a classical conflict with authority.

It was obviously a place where I would have to tread very lightly as Peter's therapist, since I was now clearly cast in the role of enemy stepfather, as well as loving father. So I decided I would see him often, volunteer little advice or consent, make sure he received medication and rest, and wait to see if he would work out his conflict.

CHAPTER 6

Hospitalization:
Case Review and Progress

"AS SURE AS I CONVERSE with my own cells in my dreams and I become as one speaking to myself with all of the authority of my own DNA, just so sure am I of nothing—the most certain thing in the world. And I ask myself, 'cellf are you in despair?' And they say, 'No, that is only one side of what we are in. Your head is just choosing that half of the truth now, but we're still whole. Maybe your psychiatrist is crazy, but we're not!'"

I had asked Peter to begin a conversation with what he was now calling his 'cellf.' I had placed an empty chair in front of him and was using a Gestalt therapy technique he often used with his clients and had demonstrated to our training group. That excerpt was just after the role-playing of both sides of the conversation with his 'cellf.' He had turned to face me and looked in my direction without really looking at me. The thinly veiled hostility directed toward me was evident not only in this instance, but in most of his interactions with me. "...Maybe your psychiatrist is crazy, but we're not..."

I saw this start of directing hostility toward me as a healthy development. The hospitalization and medication I had prescribed had slowed Peter down. His talk and movements were slower and he was giving himself time to reintegrate some of what he had disowned. He had separated off a valued but feared part of himself —namely, his love for me, his desire to be approved by me and loved back—into a separate unit (his spirit-client) because he could not tolerate the anger he felt for me at the same time. He had created his spirit-self as a separate protected unit of his relationship to me, primarily because he could not tolerate the tremendous resentment he felt for me (and toward himself for submitting to me) which was walking hand in hand so to speak, with his love for me. This was, of course, a re-facing and in part, a re-enactment of his childhood conflict with his step-father, who vaguely reminded him of his father, whom he loved and needed and missed. At the same time, he hated the step-father because of his cruelty to his mother and brother. His associations were becoming more bizarre (as in the foregoing example) and he was slowing down and attempting to reintegrate this disowned part of himself. That particular excerpt was from the session we had five days after his entry into the hospital.

Then, immediately after that session, he became extremely withdrawn. When I saw him on the next two days, he spoke not one word. The third day after (eighth day in the hospital), the ward attendant gave me the following two poems found in the day room. The first was found in the morning, the second in the afternoon. They were unsigned and untitled, but in Peter's handwriting.

Poem No. 1

As I got older
More hair grew on my chest
And occasionally I pulled on it
And pulled some out.
My hand got redder
And my thumb got to
Looking different to me

By the time I planned
     Things
     I thought
"Ah, what's the use?"

Now I'm older still.
There are some gray hairs showing there
But I can do whatever I fancy.
I can see that over the hill I'll soon

Be tired of both doing and fancying.
Maybe something neither dope or
Meditation can cure.

Poem No. 2

This strange unconscious
creature that dwells me.

Grunts and moans my life
its way.
I'm tired of strumbling with us...
Let's all join come and hand
in one big circle together

No.
The best one can hope for is
a cease-fire and an early truce
for there'll be no marriage here
except in death...
as usual.

Those poems represent a transition state —a kind of slowing down and entering wistfully into nihilism. Then, when I saw him on the tenth day, he resumed talking to me as though nothing had happened.

What follows next is an excerpt from dream work at the end of his tenth day in the hospital. As you will see at the end of the dream, which he interprets for himself, he starts consciously to note similarities between his 'spirit-friend' and himself.

"I dreamed of home. It was evening after a meal and people were laughing and talking. I came up behind my sister while she was standing at the sink and patted her on the ass. She said, 'Now, Mike!' (That's my brother-in-law's name). 'Quit that!' Then she turned around and saw it was me and said, 'You're not even Mike!' That's even worse!' But she was laughing and kidding and having a good time. Jimmy, my brother, was rolling a joint and there was a wood stove there. Someone at the table asked me where I was going next and I said I didn't know, but I thought it was about time to leave. (I felt like I'd been there a couple of weeks). Then the idea seemed to come to me in the dream, 'you're traveling—make your way south for the winter.' So I went into the dining room again and the table had been cleared and everyone was looking at a map of the United States. I walked through the door singing a line of the song 'Midnight Special.'...Well, if you ever go to Houston, boy, you better walk right...' and I told them I was headed for Florida and Houston, because that's a good place to go to when it's winter..."

(Long pause.)

"...There was happiness and yearning in that dream. A happiness and a yearning ..."

(Quiet again.)

"God, I would like to go home. Make a home. Have a home... There must be millions of us. We all want to go home ...where it's warm ... for the winter. So we're about to leave home to get there. Poor, dumb us ... lots of roads are crowded and lots of houses are empty. And we all want to go home."

(Quiet again.)

"That dream has helped me understand my spirit-friend a little better. I understand his yearning to have a body...to be located in one place. It must be terribly lonely for him, spread out all over the place at one time like that. He wants a home. Poor Bastard. I'd let him live in mine, my body, except I've got a spirit of my own there that's already too contentious for anyone to get along with. And the first time he really wanted something I didn't, I just know he'd pull in extra power on me, and there I'd be."

He was quiet for a long time. So I repeated the last phrase.

"... And there I'd be ..."

" What?"

"And there I'd be ... was the last thing you said."

"Oh. I thought you were talking about yourself."

Here again was an entry into the fruitful confusion, which unified Peter and his spirit-friend and myself and the other loved/hated father figures in his life. However, the situation was such that if I gave this interpretation at this *point, he wouldn't be able to accept it, because I was a principal figure in his internal power struggle. For me to 'explain' anything at this point was simply to ensure that he would reject my interpretation. So I sat quietly. In fact, sitting quietly was about all I did for the next three weeks.*

After about two weeks, Peter confessed that he was no longer in communication with his spirit- friend and in fact, had not been since his entry into hospital. After that, for about a week, there was a very gloomy period and he fell asleep occasionally during therapy sessions. Then at the beginning of the eighth week, the following dream emerged.

"I dreamed I was in a room with three men standing around a table raised up higher than me. One of them said of me — partly to me, and to the others, ' What a strange, persistent little Sir ... only one Armageddon to face and preparing for it 30,000 times ...' (Partly chiding me, but amused and at the same time patting me on the head.) 'Strange little creature."

Peter's own interpretation of this was: "...I'm learning how to be amused at my own worry-making self. I'm all the characters in that dream. I think it means I've seen myself through the eyes of a transcendent spirit and so I don't take myself so seriously anymore."

I agreed with Peter's interpretation and I also added that I thought the recurrence of the number three was meaningful.

That the three men might represent father, stepfather and me, as we had been incorporated and 'raised up' to a higher level by Peter and had become the 'three in one' (father, son and Holy Ghost) spirit. I added that as he became surer of our acceptance of him, he would be more capable of understanding the supportive criticism we sometimes represented. He agreed with me. He didn't resist. Neither did he over-react. "I think you're right." And then he was quiet for a long time.

Having been listened to, understood and agreed with encouraged me. Over the next two weeks, I risked a few more interpretations. At the end of ten weeks, I decided that his improvement had been good enough that he could leave the hospital, continue in individual therapy with me and continue in his intern group, although, he was, of course, still relieved of his therapeutic duties with patients in the hospital and out-patient clinic. We made an explicit agreement that once he had left the hospital he would continue to take his medication as prescribed.

My decision to let him continue in the intern group was based on a number of considerations, some of which are extraneous to this book. The primary reason however was that I considered this group the best context for Peter to develop and work out what had now become his focused anger towards me. I also wanted to use him to train other therapists. The following excerpt is from the end of an intern group session three weeks after he left the hospital. His anger at this point was directed toward one of the other male interns who was pressing him on the issue of whether he had been lying or not about what had been going on with him since he entered the hospital. He was still on medication at this time, but it had been decreased to less than one third of the initial dosage.

"...Of course I deceived Myerson! I'm not stupid. I may be crazy as some of you think. But I'm not stupid. If you end up in a mental hospital and you want to get out, you behave however you have to in order to get out. Namely, you figure out what your Doctor's interpretation of your illness is, have the cure emerge from you in bits and pieces 'spontaneously,' pull it all together to make him feel brilliant, stop mentioning whatever it was that got you in there—in my case my spirit-friend—and get the hell out. Anybody who would stay in a goddamn mental hospital is crazy! I know and you know—some of you know anyway—most funny-farms are a pile of shit! This one included. The hospital doctors are even worse than Myerson. In fact, they're usually a bunch of retarded assholes who couldn't make it in the private practice of general medicine—or couldn't speak English when they got run out of any one of a dozen countries with the rest of the corrupt fascists supported by our wonderful CIA, the largest terrorist organization on earth—and who would have a mental breakdown if they didn't have walls of an institution to wrap around them and hold them up!"

"The best evidence I have of my sanity is that I was cool enough to lie and split that shit-hole, you dumb bastards! Any sane man could see that!"

"But it worked, by God, no matter how cool I was. Myerson,

you're a son-of-a-bitch, for your helpful little trick of helping me into the hospital! I got knocked on my ass with tranquilizers and lost track of my spirit-friend. And don't think I don't resent it. I do! I slept a lot but when I was going to sleep or waking up—the halfway place where I usually carried on whole discourses with my spirit-friend—that place was simply a drug stupor. And I found myself trying so hard to overcome it, I started imagining the conversations and I knew that wouldn't do, goddamn it! Or I would go fucking crazy! So I stopped trying, slept and decided to haul my ass out of that hospital."

"The only reason I let Myerson think he was helping, was to avoid a 'discharge from voluntary commitment against Doctor's advice' on my record and because I wanted to stay in this internship program. But I'm not much interested anymore. Fuck this program! I want my spirit back—my friend, my teacher, my one who helped me by my help of him. Screw you guys! Screw all of you— and especially you, Myerson—I'm splitting!"

With that statement, he stood up and stormed out of the room. So ended Peter's participation in the post doctoral intern program. Except for one additional private session after he had cooled down a bit, it was also the end of my therapeutic contact with him. He had left home again.

CHAPTER 7
Conclusions and Theoretical
Issues Raised by the Case

t HIS CASE REVIEW has been presented in hopes that my work with this patient and my interpretation of the work could demonstrate the validity of two apparently opposite schools of thought in the field of psychiatry. One school of thought we will call "classical" and, although outright explicit advocates of this position as I will describe it are few, it is still the most influential in the current treatment of mental illness. In the course of the evolution of psychiatric theory and practice, we have come to believe in specific diagnostic and treatment procedures. We believe that mental illness can be treated. We believe there are a limited number of kinds of mental illness. In fact, there are a number of fairly discreet categories and sub-categories. Most forms of mental illness fit into these categories. Professionals, who care for people who are mentally ill, know the treatment procedures thus far developed for the types of mental illness the categories represent.

Roughly, these are the beginning distinctions, followed by the trail down the branches of the tree to Peter's diagnosis: there are two global categories for mental disturbances: neuroses and psychoses. Under psychoses, one sub-category is Schizophrenia. One sub-category under Schizophrenia is Paranoid. Another classification under that is "Delusions of Grandeur." Peter X, according to this diagnostic system, is a Paranoid (pursued and haunted by and in pursuit of a spirit) Schizophrenic (about which he has opposite and conflicting thoughts and feelings) with Delusions of Grandeur (and for whom he takes on the delusion of bearing the burden of being a transcendent being's therapist).

Another implicit-by-agreement tenet of the classical school is that Schizophrenia is a relatively permanent, though treatable, for control, state of being. One is schizophrenic pretty much for life, but with chemicals and care one can keep the illness under control.

The other school of thought, represented by the so-called radicals among us, such as R.D Laing and Thomas Szasz, says that the categories we've developed blind us to the person and inevitably make us condescend, in an inhuman and unhelpful way, to the classified no-longer-human being and treat him and study him like a bug in a test-tube. Furthermore, says this school of thought, Schizophrenia should be seen as a developmental stage of growth, taking varying amounts of time to complete. If left to run its course, and not interfered with either chemically or therapeutically by meddling professionals it usually will resolve itself. It is not a permanent disease and should not, in fact, be called a disease at all. (See *The Myth of Mental Illness* by Thomas Szaz)

I wish to talk about Peter's case, first, in terms of a meaning both schools can agree upon—what we'll call "deviations from consensus reality." Powerful emotions, and in this case mainly anger, provide energy that can be used for creative distortions of reality. When these distortions become a sort of global set with which one construes the world, and when one becomes obsessed with a way of conceptualizing things—and even a way of literally seeing things—that condition is what we call psychosis. It came about in Peter's case as a transmission of rage which he felt toward his "fathers;" his biological father who died and deserted him at the age of six, his step-father who beat his mother and brother and him and treated him cruelly, and his brother-in-law who was overly strict with him for the two years Peter lived in his home, me and possibly others. The re-emergence of this rage in the supervisory situation was triggered by the heavy workload of patients whose troubles he took too much to heart and the requirement that he "submit" to me in a training analysis.

Peter had what I consider to be a psychotic break. However, please note that (1) the episode had a beginning, middle and end. Schizophrenia in this instance may be considered a lifelong "potential" but not a lifelong disease. The psychosis itself can be classified as temporary; (2) his case was what I would call a "mild" psychosis. It was resolved when (with the aid of drugs and hospitalization and rest, which any good "classical" psychiatrist would prescribe) he re-directed his energies and focused his rage on me, and in fact the whole psychiatric profession. I was blamed for the loss of his psychosis. That, I take as confirmation that a real change occurred and as a compliment.

Leaving the group and resigning from the program were realistic steps which he took to manifest his anger toward me and they represented also, I think, a realistic self-evaluation with regard to his future participation in the program.

In conclusion, what I am proposing is that we not throw out the baby with the bathwater in the field of psychiatry. We grow by making modifications. The modifications I propose are that we qualify, but not throw away our use of diagnostic categories, by designating the power and intensity of the illness, such as mild, intermediate, and intensive. Secondly, we make a clear distinction in every case, particularly in psychoses, between "episode" and "potential" so that there is a more explicit recognition that there is room for change within the confines of our categories. Thirdly, we should become more accepting of the view, as many of our colleagues on the "left" encourage us to, that re-emergence of violent emotions with some patients is a development leading out of psychosis, rather than further evidence of a demented state.

These revisions are particularly important in the light of instances of "spiritual" types of aberrations, which are on the increase with the religious fads that young people participate in these days, as well as cases of psychotic episodes which are chemically induced and temporary, although intensive. It may be, as some have predicted, that we are entering a new age of "spiritual" psychoses, and those of us who work on the front lines of the profession had better be ready.

Victor Myerson, M.D.

Editor's Postscript

The contents of this book were a part of an intensive panel presentation to the American Psychiatric Association at the Annual Convention in October 1995. It was originally intended as an example of how a rapprochement might be creatively accomplished between the "left" and the "right" membership in our Association. As things turned out, it apparently added to the controversy, but in the discussions which followed, everyone sharpened their intellectual tools a bit.

It was out of this experience and with the encouragement of members of the Association that Dr. Myerson decided to publish the case and the discussion in book form, in hopes that it might be a gratifying experience for others in the professional community of healthcare workers and laymen. This condensation leaves out much of Dr. Myerson's discussion of the case, while leaving in, hopefully, just enough to get across his point of view, and his contribution to the profession.

Brad Blanton, Ph.D., editor

BOOK II

THE ETERNAL SPLIT-SECOND SOUND-LIGHT BEING
A review in three parts of
The Case of Peter X

By

PETER HOWARD, PH.D.

(Reprinted with permission from *The New York Review of Books*)

A Review in Three Parts of The Case of Peter X

INSTALLMENT NO.1

THE BEING

September 10th, 1997

MY NAME IS PETER HOWARD. I am the man identified as Peter X in Dr. Victor Myerson's book, *The Case of Peter X: A Model Case of Paranoid Schizophrenia with Delusions of Grandeur. The New York Review of Books* has agreed to publish this review of *The Case of Peter X*, even though I, the reviewer, am the subject of the book. This is the first of three installments, and I ask you in the beginning to reserve your judgment until you've read the entire review.

The Case of Peter X, is a good, maybe even brilliant book. It's surprising success as a popular book is due, I think, to Dr. Myerson's clarity and simplicity of expression and skillful interpretive ability. I have the utmost respect for Dr. Myerson. I respect him not only for his clarity and for being an astute and comprehensive scholar and a good psychiatrist, but also for his courage to venture out among his avaricious colleagues into the midst of controversy seeking to make peace. He knew when he first made his presentation of this case before the American Psychiatric Association that he was risking challenges all along the line. His diagnosis, treatment procedure and especially his conclusions and proposed theoretical revisions made him a target for both the left wing and right wing in psychiatry. When he published the small book, he was opening the way to such challenges in the public arena rather than just within the close confines of professional colleague-ship and he deserves honor and respect for doing so.

Just what did he propose? He said that his patient, Peter X, was a "mild" paranoid schizophrenic with delusions of grandeur, that in the course of treatment, including hospitalization and drug therapy along with psychotherapy, there was a remission of the psychotic state via re-focusing of aggressive anger energy toward the therapist and withdrawal of that energy from the delusional system developed by the patient at the onset of the psychotic episode. Now that all seems fairly straightforward; but, being the meticulous man he is about being fair and open to criticism, he gave his colleagues a large sampling of the raw data from which he drew his conclusions. That is a risk not many professionals are willing to leave themselves open for. Let me quote from a few other recent reviews of the book, to show you what I mean.

"... *The dictionary-definition of Sociopath is a perfect description of Peter X. the supposedly formerly 'psychotic' patient in Dr. Myerson's book.*" —Fred Lees, MD.

"*I agree with Dr. Myerson's diagnosis: this man is a paranoid schizophrenic with delusions of grandeur—I say 'is' rather than 'was' because I disagree with Myerson's conclusion, based on scanty evidence and hope, that there was a cure. The patient left in the middle.*"—Hans Shriver, MD., LL.D

"*The patient, Peter X, is and probably always was perfectly sane—a little spirited perhaps, but sane. Perhaps his psychiatrist is crazy.*" —T.R. Crews, MD.

The variety of responses like these (and there are others), although confusing, was in a way predictable. In the field of psychotherapy, and in many other borderline art/science fields, there is an inverse relationship between the amount of data provided and the amount of agreement about its meaning. In other words, the more information available the greater the disagreement.

What I wish to say in this review is not so much a part of this general field of argument as it is a separate and wholly other perspective. For, in the final analysis, not only is Dr. Myerson correct, but so are his critics. I agree with them all. They are all quite right about me. Quite right.

Dr. Myerson has given the reasons for his diagnosis in the book, and I find no fault with them. That I am sane, as Dr. Crews suggests is equally clear to me. That I am sociopathic is borne out by the manipulation evident in my life-story, my associations to my life story in the book and in my manipulative way of getting out of the mental hospital. And it is supported by the further confession I now am about to make.

I actually saw Dr. Myerson two times after that last group session mentioned in the book. I gave him permission in writing to use my case history for the APA presentation and for the book. I looked over the manuscript and agreed with him to his face, even in his conclusion that what in fact had gone on was the remission of a psychosis. (Only a sociopath would say that, knowing it was such a small piece of the truth it was false.) But before we go into that, I would like to play a bit of a game with you and start over again and review Dr. Myerson's book in a way similar to the way he reviewed me.

The book is O.K. but not really sensational. Were I not the main subject I would not be as interested as I am. My first criticism of the book is that like most documents of its kind, it's a bit boring. My criticism of Dr. Myerson is only one, and a simple one at that. But it's one all of the other reviewers so far have missed: namely, *he never really listened with an open mind. Not once, in the entire book does he take up consideration of the literal content of what I said.* His theoretical interpretations are as watertight and well reasoned as such things can be, but he forgot to listen to what I was saying. He *heard only what he thought what I was saying represented.* Not only did he not hear me, his patient, but he obviously didn't 'hear' Ronald Laing, the man who really prompted the writing of the book itself, because what Laing says is, as literally as you can, observe and listen, at least every now and then, with your theoretical tools suspended, so you can get the patient's point of view of what's going on.

So I bring a very serious charge against my former psychiatrist, because if what I have said is true, (and I quote him here as the authority), "when distortions become a sort of global set with which one construes the world and one becomes obsessed with a way of conceptualizing things—that condition is what I call psychosis." (Page 52), he's crazy.

What possibly made him stop listening to me early in the game was that he over-identified with me (his projection that my illness was caused by over-identification with my patients) and became angry with me because I challenged his authority. What he has been used to now for years, is being sucked up to by a bunch of still-wet-behind-the-ears, fresh out of medical school youngsters who want to grovel, get certified, haul ass and make some money without rocking the boat. That's the truth. I, he admits, was an exception.

That's enough; I don't want to write a whole book to make a minor point. Take my word for it, or don't; everything I've just said is true. Everything Myerson said was true too. What his other critical reviewers have said is correct, as well. And of course, it's all bullshit.

So now, when we get that it's all bullshit, we're thrown back on Occam's razor, so to speak. So now I'm going to tell you the simplest truth. (Not that this isn't bullshit too. It's just that all of us so-called sane humans have agreed to work with the general principle that the simplest explanation is the best.) So here it is. What I propose to do here is to provide an alternative explanation of my behavior. I agree to fight fair. I'll be just as rational as Myerson and his critics—that you can judge for yourself—but hear me out. I want to tell you the story of what happened to me during that time.

I have admitted that I was lying in order to get out of the hospital when I agreed with Dr. Myerson that his version of the truth was correct. Well, I was lying! Furthermore, *I had already re-established contact with the Eternal Split-Second Sound-Light Being before I got out of the hospital and have, in fact, continued to communicate with him over the course of the last year and a half.*

The day after I entered the hospital, I was forced, as all patients are, to go before a group of psychiatrists and trainees at the hospital and participate in a "staff review." I had been heavily tranquilized (because the doctors were nervous about having to "review" a former colleague, and when doctors are nervous, patients get more tranquilizers in order to calm the nerves of the staff), but I was *still* angry about the whole degrading process. Being an uncreative lot, they proceeded in the same way with me exactly as I had proceeded along with them in the past several months with other patients, to ask the rote questions one asks when the preliminary diagnosis has been schizophrenia. And one of the first things the patient is asked to do is to interpret some proverb and if he interprets in some way consistent with the doctors, he's sane, and if he fails, he's either crazy or mentally retarded. So, one oaf, with whom I had several previous run-ins, asked rather officiously, "Dr. Howard, what is the meaning of the phrase—'Birds of a feather, flock together'?"

Swimming up out of the drug fog in all the good energy of my anger, I answered him. "Well," I said, "where you find one son-of-a-bitch, you find four or five of the bastards!" Nobody laughed. They evidently didn't get it. I demonstrated the ability to do analogical thinking, got the meaning of a proverb, while at the same time shaming them and damning them for their ignorance. Ignoring that, if they noticed at all, they trudged on. They proceeded pro forma to ask what day it was, who was president, etc. Eventually, they wrote on my chart that speedy but familiar little classification in mental hospitalese, "disoriented as to time and space." They did this in complete contradiction to the evidence that said I knew where I was in linear time. Again they were demonstrating that once a conspiracy of minds is committed to a diagnosis, all evidence to the contrary is simply considered to be inapplicable. It's pretty common and it's pretty much the same as the Salem witch trials.

That phrase, "disoriented as to time and space," is one with which we lightly skip over the fundamental question of our age: Time. And now it is time to face that. I want to share the perspective on time I learned from my friend and colleague, the Eternal Split-Second Sound-Light Being. Here it is.

There are three kinds of time: linear time, cyclical time, and eternal time.

Linear time is dates and plans, one hour after the next, day after day, year after year, as life as we know it goes on and history unfolds (the kind of time people should be oriented to in order to escape mental hospitals).

Cyclical time is moon-time, women's period time, Arnold Toynbee cycles in history time, seasonal change, recurrence and repetition time

Eternal time is pointed to by anything that happens an infinite number of times like waves—something so forever it's always taken for granted. When the infinite recurrence of waves becomes as one we have an analogical experience of eternal time—something that precedes and follows linear time and includes all kinds of time within it but really has no beginning and no end.

And there are two kinds of *space*, which make up any human's life-space: space *internal* and space *external*.

Space internal may not be an actual space, but we have nothing else to call it—it's where we are with our eyes closed, or in sleep, or in our almost limitless imaginations.

Space external is whatever space is relevant to life maintenance procedures for any animal—as John Bleibtreu says in *The Parable of the Beast*, it's different for eagles then it is for earthworms. The external life of an earthworm is different from that of an eagle and both are different than that of a fish. That space external, by the way, is not only different for different species of animals *it may be not the same for every human person.*

So we have three times and two spaces. Three times two equals six ways to be confused and still be right—or infinitely wrong—and which is what's really terrifying—to not know whether you're completely lost or not. This is also why my 'psychosis' is a theological statement—a theory about how to say yes to more than just one small part of life. (Because hospitals and doctors don't actually know about time, there is no real use in staying there for true time and space cadets.) Suffice it to say, for the time being, that *the perspective of eternal time is the context in which all other time occurs.* And it is the perspective, ultimately, that explains all this.

Now I will tell you what happened to me after I left the hospital and the training program.

After I left the post-doctoral internship program, I went back to Greece, to an island where I had lived for a while before. It was there that I had my first extensive direct contact with the Sound-Light Being. And there we talked to my 'cellf' again (Here is the weakest part of my argument, dear reader. I cannot tell you how I know the difference between authentic contact with the other, and a hallucination, but when the hospital was driving me crazy, I knew.) I also knew, at least, that even if insane, I preferred my personal insanity to the one they claimed to share in common.

Contact came again when I was copying and re-editing my review of John Bleibtreu's book, which Vic Myerson had, apparently inadvertently, given me. I was copying excerpts and making notes to myself. What follows is the exact trail I went down. I was recording the story, in detail, of the life cycle of one of nature's more enigmatic parables, the hapless cattle tick ...

"*The cattle tick is a small, flat-bodied, blood-sucking arachnid with a curious life history. It emerges from the egg not yet fully developed, lacking a pair of legs and sex organs. In this state it is still capable of attacking cold-blooded animals such as frogs and lizards, which it does. After shedding its skin several times, it acquires its missing organs, mates, and is then prepared to attack warm-blooded animals. After mating, the male soon dies.*

"*The eyeless female is directed to the tip of a twig on a bush by her photo-sensitive skin, and there she stays through darkness and light, through fair weather and foul, waiting for the moment that will fulfill her existence. In the Zoological Institute, at Rostock, prior to World War I, ticks were kept on the ends of twigs, waiting for this moment for a period of eighteen years. The metabolism of the creature is sluggish to the point of being suspended entirely. The sperm she received in the act of mating remains bundled into capsules where it, too, waits in suspension, until mammalian blood reaches the stomach of the tick, at which time the capsules break, the sperm are released and they fertilize the eggs which have been reposing in the ovary, also waiting in a kind of time suspension.*

"The signal for which the tick waits is the scent of butyric acid, a substance present in the sweat of all mammals. This is the only experience that will trigger time into existence for the tick.

"The tick represents, in the conduct of its life, a kind of apotheosis of subjective time perception. For a period as long as eighteen years nothing happens. The period passes as a single moment: but at any moment within this span of literally senseless existence, when the animal becomes aware of the scent of butyric acid, it is thrust into a perception of time, and other signals are suddenly perceived.

"The animal then hurls itself in the direction of the scent. The object on which the tick lands at the end of this leap must be warm; a delicate sense of temperature is suddenly mobilized and so informs the creature. If the object is not warm, the tick will drop off and re-climb its perch. If it is warm, the tick burrows its head deeply into the skin and slowly pumps itself full of blood. . . ."

". . . The extraordinary preparedness of this creature for that moment of time during which it will re-enact the purpose of its life contrasts strikingly with the probability that this moment will ever occur. There are doubtless many bushes on which ticks perch, which are never by-passed by a mammal within range of the tick's leap. As do most animals, the tick lives in an absurdly unfavorable world —at least so it would appear to the compassionate human observer. But this world is

merely the environment of the animal. The world it per-
ceives—which experimenters at Rostock called its Umwelt,
its perceptual world—is not at all unfavorable. During this
period, it is apparently unaware of temperature changes.
Being blind, it does not see the leaves shrivel and fall and then
renew themselves on the bush where it is affixed. Unaware of
time it is also unaware of space, and the multitudes of forms
and colors, which appear in space. It waits, suspended in
duration for its particular moment of time, a moment distin-
guished by being filled with a single, unique experience; the
scent of butyric acid.

"Though we consider ourselves far removed as humans
from such a lowly insect-form as this, we too are both aware
and unaware of elements which comprise our environment. We
are subjectively aware of the aging process; we know that we
grow older, that time is shortened by each passing moment. For
the tick, however, this moment that precedes it's burst of voli-
tional activity, the moment when it scents butyric acid and is
thrust into purposeful movement, is close to the end of its time.
When it fills itself with blood, it drops from its host, lays its
eggs, and dies.

Tick. . . Tock.

"Over the course of our evolutionary journey we have
gained an incredible intellectual heritage; we have contrived
a system of comprehending causal relations and recreated our
ecological environment, but we have lost as well. On the simplest, most pragmatic level, this loss becomes obvious when we

must provide special "survival schools" for downed airmen, deprived of their civilization, so that they may learn how to survive——simply to exist, to sustain life——in a world which their primitive ancestors found sustaining, and which sustained those previous stages of man's metamorphosis for hundreds of millions of years. This scrim of culture has blurred our perception of the natural Umwelt; this blurring, loss of contact is symbolized by a lack of knowledge of how to do certain things, such as how to make a fire without matches. But the real loss is far more extensive."

"We have lost whole areas of experience. We are, in effect, numb to them, as the tick, having evolved the specialized conduct of its life, is numb to the very passage of time. We have lost, in general terms, a sense of intimacy with the cosmos, an innate knowledge of our belonging to and with all the living forms that swarm thickly on and through the surface of our planet. We have lost our ability to exist harmoniously within the solar system and within the cosmos at large."

After that passage, I wrote this note, and I began to feel strange bodily sensations as I did so.

"And now if we discover our loss——if we really take this seriously and become aware of that which we previously possessed, that's perhaps the first step to the return of our origin—— the beginning of our re-enlightenment,——to know our losses."

Then as I continued to copy Bleibtreu's further comments I became light headed.

"As man evolved the symbolic language of speech, he lost, to a great extent, his ability to converse with his environment in the language of direct experience. This loss has occurred because we have trained our intellect to intervene between ourselves and experience. We have lately discovered there are forces abroad in the world to which animals respond. At one time or another in our evolutionary history we, too, responded to these forces. They now remain mostly vestigial like the twenty-eight day lunar cycle of human female menstruation. We once lived much more intimately with the moon and experienced its influence more directly upon our activities. This new mythology (science) which is being derived from the most painstaking research into other animals, their sensations and behavior, is an attempt to re-establish our losses—to place ourselves anew within an order of things, <u>because faith in an order is a requirement of life.</u>...."

". . . Once we then acknowledge the world as being subjectively perceived, we must also acknowledge that the world varies with an individual's given sensibilities. Are there sensibilities of which we are not now aware? Do we receive 'knowledge' of the world and the order of things from sources of sensibility that are as yet inaccessible to the intellect? Every myth, including this new one, (science) maintains that we do, and that what we call intuition is a response to these sources of intelligence; that the acknowledgment of the 'reality' of intu-

ition is an indispensable part of the dialogue of experience."
(John Bleibtreu, The Parable of the Beast, *Pages 3-8)*

Then, as I wrote down these quotes I had collected from guru Nanak and other teachers, my heart began to race.

"The Lord who has given life to the entire creation,
Who is a supreme Giver, who nurtures and sustains everyone,
Resides within the human frame. . . ."

". . . Our body is not merely a cave in which to contain the soul;
It also holds the Indescribable
And infinite Lord within it. . . ."

". . . Within the body resides the unknowable One;
But those who are foolish and proud think they know the Truth,
And search for him without."

Guru Nanak

"This very place the lotus paradise
This very body the Buddha."

Unknown

"He whom you have tried to find in the four corners of the earth
He is within; you fail to see Him because He lives
Behind the veil of illusion."

Kabir Sahib

"The Lord dwells within this human temple. We are very foolish not to go to the place where we can find Him. Instead, we run around in circles. We retire to forests, to mountain caves or to mosques or temples, but never succeed in finding Him. Between us and the Lord there is a blinding screen of illusion, and that is why we are unable to see Him."

> *Charan Singh*
> *Divine Light, page 32*

I added then one note again..."The Sufi's and Buddhists and Hindu's agree on the mystery that can be known, but not understood."

I felt strange again, as if on some precipice. Nevertheless I continued to copy notes and write, pulling everything together, because I felt all my bodily reactions were from the power of the meaning of the words that were forming in my mind.

In his book, *Theoretical Biology*, von Uexhull wrote:

"All psychic processes, feelings, and thoughts are invariably bound to a definite moment and proceed contemporaneously with objective sensations ..." *(the italics are mine.)*

When John Bleibtreu speaks of the cattle tick, and von Uexhull's theory of all processes being bound to moments, which are either "accented" through noticing or "unaccented" because not experienced, they are in complete agreement.

"Time envelopes both the subjective and objective worlds in the same way, and unlike space, makes no distinction between them." He defined subjective time as being a series of what he called 'moment signs'——'the smallest receptacles that, by being filled with various qualities, become converted into moments as they are lived.' Intervals of time, which do not include the kind of experience that endows them with a quality——either pain, or pleasure, or even simple attention——, he called unaccented moments. For the cattle tick, eighteen years may pass as one unaccented moment.

"For us, as we age, time appears to accelerate. For a man of middle age, a year seems to pass as swiftly as a month does for a child. Through our exposure to them, accented moment signs——those moments that contain external happenings which mobilize our resources——lose their novelty and demand less attention. We become habituated to them. Such an external happening as the sound of an airplane——which would be a moment-sign to a child, which would mobilize all his senses to integrate and evaluate this external happening——would be subliminal to an adult. Through habituation to this stimulus we would come to ignore it and the moment that was marked by its happening would be deprived of its accent. It would become unaccented. We can become no more aware than the tick of the passages of time. We are subjectively aware of the aging process; we know that we grow older, that time is shortened by each passing moment."

I was filled with wonder and energy and I wrote in my notes again: So, now and then, I, like the cattle tick, have had all this long unaccented moment, until now, in which this almost disappeared vestigial ability to *tune into the rhythm and order of the cosmos*, gets *accented* and people like me regress back to what is now known as merely one form of insanity.

" . . . *Except ye be as little children, ye shall not enter the kingdom of heaven. . .* "

Jesus Christ

As I wrote that last sentence, I heard laughter—and it wasn't my own. But it wasn't long before I joined in. I went back to that place of knowing called childhood in my mind—and that way of sensing through my pineal gland and my limbic brain, where my heart and mind are integrated—and like the smell of butyric acid for the cattle tick, it triggered a leap and I became a sounding light, in touch with that world which is always there. And in that Eternal Split-Second, the Sound-Light Being returned.

A Review in Three Parts of The Case of Peter X

ínsʈALLMEnʈ nO.2

THE
CONVERSATION

October 2, 1997

HE SOUND-LIGHT BEING came back to me laughing. Even though I am one of you. Even though what I am about to say is true of us, he came back to me, laughing. He was happy to finally be telling me what I had always known—what you and I know but don't let on about—that our heads have destroyed our faith. All we've got in common anymore are those instruments of destruction called minds and our watches. When we start to escape our alienation we become at once more grounded and connected to the earth and in our bodies and at the same time more transcendent, free of our watches, beyond time as we've known it. There is a difference inside me and inside you between our imaginary selves (who we think we are) and the whole full being that we are—that "me" which is my mind and my body and the light I have begun to call my "cellf." Kazantzakis is right. He says, "God is a potter; he works in mud."

The Sound-Light Being and I want to tell you something. What we've been trying to tell you is that we all may be vaguely aware of the life of the spirit beyond what we're used to in this body. That we all may have another sense organ that all of our life is not just in this body but also beyond the cycles of our heartbeat and our breathing and the ringing in our ears and the circulation of energy. Beyond all these bodily cycles and beyond the mental machinations supported by these cycles, there is a life of the spirit, a world of the spirit, that is within but also transcends the body, that goes beyond the limitations of the body, that is *in* but not *of* the body, and that is in but not of the world as we know it.

I'm trying to say that there is a transmitter that exists that is neutral, and that transmitter transmits to each one of us human beings through our receiver, perhaps all the cells in our bodies, and that this transmission and this reception, this transmitter and this receiver make up a single unit, or part of a whole, which is the nature of things. And to see them as transmitter and receiver is another dialectical and convenient and scientific way of believing them. And to experience them is to experience a whole-ness that in its own non-sentimental way is a gigantic permission to relax and take it easy—and come to understand that everything is in its place. And what's going on in the world, in the context of eternal time, is perfect.

When I give you these conversations between the Sound-Light Being and me, the dialogue is written as if we are two separate beings, and we are. But it's more like two lights signaling each other in Morse code, powered by the same generator.

I am in love with the light. I think we all are. The light in the eyes of any person, even those whose psyche has been mutilated, excites my whole being like a child's smile. An "ugly'" woman with the light is more fun to make love to than a vain goddess with blank eyes. The real goddess is love. Goddess is love.

These new conversations weren't therapy sessions or any such superficial game as we had played in the beginning. They were debates of the heart in which we were both vitally involved. We were being both patient and therapist.

We talked about the despair of existential life and the despair of being trapped in eternal time. The despair of being trapped in a body and the despair of being trapped in eternity. Here is what we said:

OTHER: "The last thing you said was that life was too damned hard. What's hard about it? You live in a body all the time. It keeps working until it doesn't. Tell me what it's like and what you have a hard time with."

CELLF: "I am impressed with the difficulty of making hopes come true. If hopes come true it's because we've imposed a kind of rigid structure on experience—moving forward in time so that experience of moment A is constrained in order to be relevant to experience in moment A + 1 and to have a positive result. People I work with in therapy who are self-destructive also do the same thing—they want to make sure that hopes *don't* come true so they constrain experience in order to make it relevant and to make the results negative. Really, the experience of moment A has no necessary relation to experience moment A + 1. A hope is only possible through limiting and changing and stirring. That is, it's only possible to have hopes come true when we refuse to live in the here and now. Hope seems to be built into us. At least to us earth-bound growing up humans. It's built in so tight there is great despair in trying to conquer hope. Hope is built in because children live in a state of 'un-satisfaction,' like hunger, and then an event occurs and they get to be in a state of satisfaction. They learn to hope for what will come. In the beginning, the world is made up of feeding events and non-feeding events. The same thing continues in growth all along and out of that experience comes the flow of language. You construct a language in that way —the end of the sentence is supposed to be behind the beginning of the sentence—and we constrain our minds so that it is possible to speak in an orderly fashion. I am aware that insofar as I try to make some hope for the future pan out, that I am depriving myself of 'me.' I am aware that the only real state—the state that is congruent with where I am and who I am, is that of being hopeless, without hope.

"So, once I get used to that idea that the natural state of being is hopelessness, the question comes: 'What does life hold in a positive sense?' And the answer traditionally has come in two ways.

One is, you make life positive, that is by constraining experience (stoically, one way or the other, as in Nietzsche and the communist, fascist and individualist experiments that have proceeded from that mind set.) The second answer is have faith that life is positive—that's the religious sense. Neither of these mean very much to me right now.

"So that's one thing. That's pretty much how I'm prisoner of my mind. The second thing is: I am a prisoner of my body. We're all prisoners of our bodies (present company excluded, of course). The aim is to make the body work for us. But even if my body is working perfectly, it's a cop-out to believe my body is working on 'my' behalf, as the self I usually consider myself to be, because my body is subject to all kinds of time/space pressures. My body gets tired, my body gets hungry, and my body has to go through certain games to move from point A to B. So my body is an imperfect servant of my self, which is transcendent. And, as my body gets older, it becomes even more imperfect, it becomes a poorer and poorer servant and it becomes really a jail, more obviously a jail, and I feel more imprisoned.

"Finally, I'm plagued with the problem of meaning in relationships. I'm more aware of (than was Kierkegaard, for example) that relationships with others are defined by the conflicts and not by their congruencies. The work in relationships is to overcome the conflicts and so the definition is in terms of conflicts. Same old story, eh? I get tired of solving the same problems, just as even children weary, after a long enough time, of the same fairy tale. Or, to put it another way, I'm getting tired of problem-solving.

"So, I believe that's what human life is all about—a time/space bound operation, filled with conflict—and the assignment is basically to work within these boundaries and attempt to overcome conflict—and to get fooled every time—because the methods that one uses, that I use, to try to overcome conflicts, have to be time/space methods, so that means I have to constrict myself and therefore I lose. No matter how you try to live, in the meaning of life, you lose. Furthermore …"

OTHER: "Wait a minute. I've noticed some things I have something to say about …"

CELLF: "Sure."

OTHER: "Your argument centers around a complaint about constraint for the sake of meaning or coherence. The choice you postulate is: you can be transcendent but not coherent, or you can be coherent and time-trapped and not transcendent, but you can't be both. Right?"

CELLF: "Right."

OTHER: "So you complain, 'I can't be transcendent, trapped in my body, except to the level where hope and language take me. And when I really transcend above and beyond that, I can't be coherent.' I ask you, why is it so important to make sense out of things?"

CELLF: "…maybe it's not important. But if it's not important, then nothing is important and at the same time life is OK because then there is nothing that one is not receiving that matters. That is—talking in terms of meaning/no meaning, not in terms of satisfaction/non-satisfaction."

OTHER: "Maybe you just like to complain. You complain about the head- prison, then about the body- prison, then about the energy waste conflict-resolution-prison. If nothing really matters, you have no reason to complain, so maybe you just like it."

CELLF: "Maybe. I don't feel like it though. When I don't feel like complaining, I like that better. When I walk back and forth on this beautiful porch on the bay in the warm sun and feel the wind blowing lightly around me and at the same time spin these thoughts through my mind, my experience is dominated, but not completely, by the thoughts. I still feel warm sun on my skin. Wind in my hair. I still feel warm concrete and pieces of dirt and eggshell on my bare feet. For this gift of diversity I'm grateful to God. Still, a little something nags me. And at night, alone in the dark light of the oil lamp, not conversing with you, something is missing. And there is in me a lust, a real lust, for meaning or some such fullness and meaning is the only word label I can find for it. And there is heartbreak and fear and weariness like a wounded lover, saying over and over again to myself, 'Well, it was just not meant to be, it was just not meant to be.' And finding no consolation in it."

OTHER: "And wouldn't it be so nice if mother would come and scold you for whining?"

CELLF: "Fuck you! Maybe I did get a little sentimental. But what I was stating is fact. The transcendent self trapped in a body and a mind is unable to surpass the boundaries of the body and the mind, with any degree of regularity. But desire for a greater fullness is there in me. And if you don't like it, fuck off!

No, don't fuck off—answer me ..."

OTHER: "Well, you could stay awake in the daytime when you feel almost OK, and sleep at night."

CELLF: "On second thought, do fuck off."

OTHER: "I am sorry my laughing at you offended you, but I'm not sorry I laughed at you. Humans are funny to me and there are still many things I guess I still don't understand about experience in a whole life in a body, just visiting across the line occasionally as I do. You speak of the despair of knowing too much with your head and not having forgotten the knowledge of the heart from when you were a child, but somehow having stopped in advance. Your head is bigger than your heart. The argument you use constrains experience unnecessarily. 'What is wrong with constraining experience?' I've asked you, and you answered, 'Well, it limits me and it hurts.' If you have any defense for yourself in being a bit sentimental in the negative direction, then use it to support me when I suggest you slant your resolve to emote just a bit in the other direction. For example, couldn't you just usually live in '*cellf wonderstanding*?' It's not ordered and clear to explain but explanations there are not important. You have a desire for more—more wholeness—more meaning. You desire more. But I know that you know of a space where you understand that nothing really matters and nothing really does matter. And there, you don't have to have hope or anything else. In that space, nothing, including desire, really matters, and that's fine."

CELLF: "But, if nothing really matters, then the essence of being, of perceiving and apprehending those experiences, is wiped out, because in apprehending the experience there is an energy flow, and the energy flow—if it doesn't matter, is just final irony—that you should be conned into spending energy on something that doesn't matter."

OTHER: "…Only you're holding on to some kind of idea of meaning—because you interpret it as a con only in the light of holding on to some kind of idea of meaning. You believe that the essence of being is perceiving and apprehending experience. You wish to be in transcendent space and understand it all in linear terms. For me, there are two ways of being in that transcendent space—one is feeling completely neutral—as though I were objective—and nothing really matters. The other is being in that space and feeling good. I've been in that space both ways and it seems to me there is nothing different conceptually about the space. And there is nothing different experientially about the space itself when I visit it as a bodily experience in someone's body, except that I feel full, warm, loving one time, and another I feel absolutely neutral."

CELLF: "Well, another time you can feel as I do—dead, empty, drained in a sense, and at other times there is ecstasy, a sense of the umbrella, the endless umbrella. It seems to me that being in that transcendent space, you pick and choose from an unlimited range of being-space, and surface with the ones you happen to be inclined to surface with."

OTHER: "But the point of transcendence is that they are all inter-valent, equal—everything's there, but you are content to let it be. The space I'm talking about is beyond desire, so maybe we're not talking about the same space. Cellf-wonderstanding is a given in the space I'm talking about."

CELLF: "Yes, and maybe you just can't understand because you don't really know what pain mixed with memory in a body is like."

OTHER: "Maybe, and maybe you're just like a Jew or an Orthodox Christian: 'You couldn't possibly understand, because you aren't chosen (or special, or saved) like me.' To quote a friend, fuck you!"

CELLF: "Well, by God, you don't have a body, or a lifetime of experience in a body of your own to go by and it may not be the same. Don't bitch at me. It's not my fault. I'll be happy to pray for you, though."

OTHER: "I won't condescend to even reply to that. Stick to the point. Let's assume you can, as you say, surface into transcendent space with any feeling base you are inclined to. Why don't you choose? Answer this simple question for me: Why don't you choose to live in bliss?"

CELLF: "'Living in bliss' isn't possible for me because I'm self-aware. I live in a unique recipe of memory—the features were kind of chosen out of a grab-bag a long time ago and put together to create my character. These features have to do, I think, beyond anything else, with being self-aware. My earliest memories which go back to the time when I was a year and a half old, have to do with—'I am Peter, I live with mom and dad in ...' The item of self-awareness is just too deeply built in, I think, for me to give it up. I think people can live as long as they live in innocence—and the prime thing they have to be innocent of is themselves. As long as they can do that, they are just fine, because the meaning that is attached to self-awareness isn't part of the equation—isn't part of what is going on. And, therefore, meaning can be shifted and the meaning of meaning absent.

Shifting meaning is, of course, the thing that politicians do but we all do it too in the politics of our own life. We constantly make the meaning shift. I move from sensuous pleasure to philosophical speculation to marriage to divorce to work to games to travel to self-improvement programs to learning Greek to despair—but self-awareness above and beyond these pre-occupations dogs my tracks like the devil. Even, I might add, into transcendent space."

OTHER: "Then you fail to transcend yourself."

CELLF: " You might put it that way. I prefer saying I cannot be who I am, that is, a being so imbued with self-awareness, and at the same time attain the innocence necessary to simply live in bliss, in those rare times, when I'm at the highest place I can get to. Innocence is by definition, not attainable. Yet it is a requirement for peace and bliss."

OTHER: "So our question really is unanswerable for both of us, though, perhaps, it's the same question. Are bliss and self-awareness in a body incompatible? I, myself, am dying to have a body. Case of curiosity killed the spirit, you might say. The difference between us is simply that you are transcendent and trapped in a body with no answer—and I am eternal with an identity and without a body and no answer to our question because I cannot fully confront the problem. The connection between us that you can translate from the light I send into language and to your embodied mind, gives us both reason to hope—oops, and there we go again."

CELLF: "Yep. Here we are again. There we go again. Back at the picture, in that place…"

Dear reader, I have nearly quit altogether in writing this just now, because it's such drivel compared to the real conversation. How can I tell you? These words are like trying to paint the beautiful rock lace fragile concrete ecstasy of an acid trip with a meat ax. What I've given you is dry bullshit. I've somehow left out our appreciation for each other. Our love for each other… All the laughing…

But then again, who in the hell are you? Readers of the goddamned *New York Review of Books!* Bunch of goddamned aged anti-fucking-war, non-activist and lost cause intellectuals. I can see you right now snickering up your sleeves, "Not only a nut, but an illiterate one to boot." Fuck you! I don't know why I waste my goddamned time. Kiss my goddamned ass, you goddamned snot nosed whiney bunch of half assed intellectuals! Postnasal drips! Shit-heads!

(The last half of this second installment was sent to *The New York Review* editor on a cassette tape with a brief, but not clear note: "If you want to print it, let your own goddamned secretaries type it." We had to call Dr. Howard to get his permission to leave out several names of people who were specifically mentioned, in a rather pejorative way at the end of Installment 2, because we were not willing to undergo the risk of libel suits from the parties involved. Permission for the changes was granted on the condition that we would insert a statement saying that we had censored Dr. Howard in this way. This is that statement. At that time, Dr. Howard said there might not be an Installment 3. We assured him that we, and we thought, our readers, were still interested. He said, "I'll see" and hung up.

The Editors

A Review in Three Parts of The Case of Peter X

ínsⱤαllmεnⱤ no.3

THE SECOND COMING

October 29th, 1997
(two weeks late ——Ed.)

E REACH CONCLUSIONS based on evidence obtained from observations using our five senses and instruments, which represent elaborations of those senses and are within the mythical context of our day called Science. That is the accepted, normal way of knowing. But it's not the only way. We have another way of telling what's going on—another way of sensing—another knowledge.

Each way of knowing has its own advantages, its own connection with time and its own despair.

Time is the key to ways of knowing. This is how we have come to understand time:

"All prey-predator relations involve competitions in linear time; the Kingfisher must be able to cut time into even smaller pieces than the trout in order to catch it in mid-passage. The Mongoose must be able to move in for the kill faster than the Cobra can recover from its strike. The Cheetah must be able to run down the Antelope, and so it goes. When we humans think about time, we usually think of it in those linear competitive terms, which are the source of anxiety. Regardless of its duration, life is still shortened by each passing moment. Elapsed time will never come again, and the great anxiety of the West is to cram each moment full of—not necessarily perception—but accomplishment." (John Bleibtreu, *Parable of the Beast,* p. 31)

This is linear time and it's to be used for accomplishing things and it's good for that. The despair of linear time is not being able to get enough or to get enough done. And of course that game is endless. Words about the despair of gluttony we are all familiar with. The answer, no matter how often the question is asked, or how many ways it is asked, is always "nothing." The question is, "What will it profit man to gain the whole world?"

By far the largest number of our technological achievements consist of devices which manipulate time in terms of something else—except, of course, for modern medicine which, by extending the life-span, quite simply and directly draws out biological time in its own terms. But, our achievements in communications and transportation—jet planes, ballistic missiles, radio and telephone, and so on—compress space in terms of linear time, thus expanding the latter. By far the largest number of machines using extrinsic power sources compress labor in terms of linear time, once again extending linear time, permitting us leisure. And that, according to the dictionary definition, is only "un-engaged time"—time for living, pure biological time.

So what's happened to us linear time freaks is we've out-smarted ourselves by getting so good at "saving"time, that we've got more than we know what to do with. Then we confront our "cellves." We get in touch with cyclical time and despair. We get back to what we lost when we got carried away with logic. We get back into cycle-logic and cycle-logical conflict. Here are yet two more quotes from John Bleibtreu:

"In biological systems, time represents the metabolic process, the absorption and utilization of energy. And seen from this point of view, time is rhythmic—the heart beat. The respiration goes in and out; time is cyclical. This is the aspect of time most important to all animals and humans, except those of us tightly in the coils of technological society. For primitive hunter-gather-er man, or even for that small section of our modern population involved in settled agriculture, the most important view of time is the cyclical one, time as measured by the passage of the seasons, the coming and going of equinoxes and solstices, though their power and influence varies with the latitude. The effects of the alteration of summer and winter, of spring and fall, are less extreme at the equator and at the poles than they are in the tem-perate zones. This succession of the seasons provides us with the great cycle we call the year. The next most important biological cycle would appear to be the twenty-eight day lunar month. Though we moderns reckon our calendars by solar months, that is really only a bookkeeping convenience. Many animal behaviors are dominated by the phases of the moon, by the cycles of its waxing and waning: more and more human behaviors and biological processes are now considered to be effected directly or indirectly by lunar periods. Of course, the smallest and most dramatic cycle, which dominates our behavior, is the diurnal period, the rotation of the earth, the alternation of night and day....

"...We know that flowers bloom in the spring, and that the swallows return to Capistrano, but as regards the conduct and apprehension of ourselves inside the phenomenon of time, we are still entranced by the fallacy of Western causal logic. The fallacy involves the idea of closed systems. *There are no closed systems in nature; everything involves everything else.*"

When I was "normal" I cared so much about being successful and saving time and not wasting time I came to understand the despair of linearity. Hospitals and psychiatrists don't know anything about time beyond what I was already in despair about. Now bear with John Bleibtreu and me a little more about cycles and then I will speak to you more personally like a sounding light from every 'cellf.' But first, try to get into the rhythm of this. Put on *Life Goes on Within You and Without You* from *Sergeant Pepper's Lonely Hearts Club Band* and listen while reading this...

"Since all living systems depend in one way or another upon our nearest star, the sun, for energy, the most universal metabolic beat is the alternation of light and dark, the diurnal rhythm. During the course of evolution organisms evolved complex variations on this basic rhythm, so the term diurnal no longer suffices to describe it. Dr. Franz Halberg of the University of Minnesota Medical School in 1959 coined a new term for this metabolic beat, and his name for it—circadian rhythm—has received wide acceptance. It is a compound word formed of two Latin roots, 'circa' meaning about, and 'dian' meaning day. The cycle of time in which all living systems exist conforms roughly to a twenty-four hour period, even though this cycle may not necessarily be clued to the alternation of light and dark. In the same way a woman's menstrual cycle conforms to the lunar period of twenty-eight days, though it need not be triggered by any particular phase of the moon." (John Bleibtreu, pp.36-37)

I have a sense of cycles within me that my mind only wonders about. That cyclical me married the wondering me.

"The tremendous contribution that botany has made to circadian rhythm studies derives from the structure of plants themselves. They have no brain, no central nervous system, yet they live their lives in conformity to cycles of time. They display behavior, they become active during the day, they sleep during the night, they bloom, and they fade. And because this activity is not directed by any system of specialized cells like a brain, or a central nervous system, the botanical approach to circadian rhythms focused on the cell itself, and on the community of cells which comprise the entire organism.

"In man as well, the feeling persists that this sense of cyclical time may not reside in the brain, nor in the central nervous system, but in all the cells of the body as they represent its parts. In the First Corinthians, Saint Paul wrote about this subject: 'The body is not one member, but many' and he defined the healthy man as one in whom 'there is no schism in the body but that all the members should have the same care for one for another.'

"The growth or development process in man—the very organization and transformation of an individual from a microscopic egg into a recognizable mammalian fetus, then into a child, and then a man—exists in time (as do all processes) but it is ordered by time, and there seems to be no conscious sense on the part of the fetus, the child, or the adolescent that any particular linear moment of time is important. The intellect does not intervene with a sense of time, as it does when we feel it is time to get up in the morning, or time to eat, or time to retire at night. Just because this ordering flow of time takes place outside consciousness, we have tended, until just recently, to ignore it." (John Bleibtreu, pp.38-39)

Okay, now listen. These days my life is like this. I get away from focusing on the real desperation of being when my curiosity grabs me. Then my curiosity goes away and I'm back into it. I'm aware that the year for me has a kind of a parent rhythm. That has to do with nature's rebirth, aging and death—which is the knowledge I was able to come close to as a child—and that has persisted on in me. It was the first thing I discovered that had some kind of integral continuity—my mother's emotional state, God knows, had no continuity—but the years do seem to have continuity and so I put a good deal of emphasis on the year—on the revival of Spring as a self-revival. So even though I know it's bullshit because the tree at moment A + 1 is also in a position relative to where it was at moment A, it's a little hard for me to swallow but I fall into it. You come to life in April. This year Spring came a little early so I came to life a little early. That's my way of setting pace—putting myself or finding myself with the natural pace.

It's been reported out of concentration camps that the last thing these people took pleasure in before they were wiped out was the natural events. This seems to make a lot of sense—because it's the thing that comes closest to making any sense—which means continuity. I have no reason for why it means anything, of course, because reason is only apprehended through language and language restricts me. Only poets come to the edge of using language to speak forth from their cellfs the full knowledge as well as the death and sweetness and pathos and despair of cycles, which we sink down into like an overstuffed chair to rest and cry.

e.e. cummings knew about it. He tells the story of the life and love of Frederick J. Anyone with a sweet maid named Annabelle Louise Noone. Anyone is everyman. Noone is everywoman. And vice versa. Fred Anyone loved Annabelle Noone and they lived and died. Which is like saying (in correct linear fashion) "Moby Dick is a story about a whale." A poet tries to be precise about that level of knowing that comes from the marriage of the head and the cellular self. This is the story of the cycles and the cycle of cycles. Fred Anyone and Annabelle Noone are forever and constantly dying. This love of anyone by no one is our story—all of us.

Anyone live in a pretty how town
with up so floating many bells down
spring summer autumn winter
he sang his didn't
he danced his did

Women and men both little and small
cared for any-one not at all
they sowed their isn't they reaped their same
sun moon stars rain

Children guessed, but only a few
as down they forgot as up they grew
autumn winter spring summer
that no-one loved him more by more

When by now and tree by leaf
she laughed his joy she cried his grief
bird by snow and stir by still
any-ones any was all to her

Someones married their everyones
laughed their crying and did their dance
sleep wake hope and then
they said their nevers they slept their dream

Stars rain sun moon
and only the snow can begin to explain
how children are apt to forget to remember
with up so floating many bells down

One day any-one died I guess
and no-one stooped to kiss his face
busy fold buried them side by side
little by little and was by was
all by all and deep by deep and more by more
they dreamed their sleep
any-one and no-one earth by April
wish by spirit and if by yes

Women and men both dong and ding
summer autumn winter spring
reaped their sowing and went their came
sun moon stars rain

That gets to me a bit even now. I feel a little sad and high. It's so good to see someone affirm something so big with such love. I'm glad I put that there. Usually, these days, I find myself indifferent to what I do or what I say because these things are really unimportant. My life cycle is a cycle among cycles. But such an affirmation of cyclical time leads me to eternity.

I find myself focusing more on the thing behind my sense of my own eminence—the thing which participates with the eminence, the I from which (or the eye from which) my spirit proceeds. And I have a clearer picture of it than most human beings do most of the time. And now I'm feeling better. So I'll go on a bit.

From another and earlier and more cyclical way of knowing I know this. The cosmos is a sign of unity, of truth, a totality of truth. It's a non-time, non-space set, and time-space are offshoots of this set. So, I Peter Howard participate in the I, the great I, the great cosmos, the great set of truth. And here in life, I, Peter Howard, have a name, which takes time to say, space to write. I am discouraged from recognizing the non-space, non-time reality of the universe by rhythms—by biological rhythms—and by linear myth which is inculcated into me very soon after I'm born. I'm resisting all modes of life now, all modes because life is arbitrary and I'm able to notice that better than most human beings. I was able to know it as an infant as well as an adult—I know it before I speak and it deters me from speaking, from reading, from using time and space. Somewhere back there I changed my mind. I didn't speak a word until I was two and a half years old. I decide prior to that I wouldn't cheapen my experience by talking like all those other fools. But I changed it because, you see, I spied some figure of me in the changing seasons, in the change of time, and I became curious about numbers. Numbers describe space and time—so I moved into that. I moved into speech, I moved into reading and into numbers. And yet, I was aware then, and I remember thinking about it then in terms that are still diffuse to me in language and yet very precise in my imagery. So I can still carry it over, somewhat grossly, into words.

So what I'm saying is that I, Peter Howard, have more carry-over than most, that allows me to see the I, the great I, as it is and me as participant in that I. All truth lies within the self. Truth lies; all within the self. No one has any parts that I don't have. I don't have any parts that others don't have. Yet, because of some psychological quirks, in failure of repression—partly psychological and partly biological—I know this wisdom still in ways that others have allowed themselves to forget. So, if I continue to stay in life, I don't know how to avoid that sense of nothing—the worn-out chess game, the finished meal, post-ejaculation depression—those are all negative to me. And I may choose not to do that—to go on in life with that perpetual sense of nothing. I listen to myself with others and there is the sense of nothing. I look at the blossoms and I say to myself—"Isn't that something," or "Isn't that something??" And yet, the exceptional blossom is the product of trained hope. The blossom has color, has shape—but it has no intrinsic beauty except that the one holding it believes it. Unless, one believes that this is beautiful, it is not beautiful. And the belief has to do with the cycle of spring, and with hope, and having learned it's the year beginning. And there are rituals and comforting myths for this because rituals copy cycles and make things easier for people to avoid their own meaninglessness. So we hold on to the blossoms…of course, meaningless as they are. We have climbed Jacob's ladder to nowhere.

It is just to the point of this question that my spirit-friend and I came. And from which, alas, we departed in two different directions. Is there a despair of eternal time? Yes, I said, because there is no hope. No, said he, because there is no hope.

I'm being a bit flip because it hurts. You may not understand, because as I've already admitted in the last installment, I failed to get across the warmth and closeness and love in our relationship. But, I'll try again, being stalwart and used to failure and despair, by providing a little background and repeating a very recent exchange between us; in fact, the most recent talk we've had.

We used to listen to music together. Particularly, Beatles' music. For a while it became almost a ritual for us to tune in on each other listening to 'life goes on within you and without you.' This last time he began with:

OTHER: "My memory is in you. In your very cells. All I have to do is tune into you and I remember and discover myself. I've learned so much from you …almost how to be human, which has really helped me more than you can imagine, to know in another way who I am… you've helped me and I appreciate you for helping me. I have become impatient and resentful, and then, less impatient and resentful. I've learned something about growing from you even from your mistakes and sometimes misplaced resentment. I've learned to let the whole easy-going flowing process of discovery take its own time to unfold and not be in a hurry about it ..."

ME: "You sound different. You sound like you're summing up ... almost like you're saying goodbye, my friend."

OTHER: "I may be. I've come to a conclusion, one that you have helped lead me to."

ME: "What is it?"

OTHER: "I think you already know. I actually discovered it while we were reading together in Dr. Myerson's book and while you were writing about us."

ME: "Well, if I know, I don't know that I know. So tell me."

OTHER: "It became clearer to me as it did to you that I have been approaching a decision with regard to our constant stuck place, where you say to me, 'You just can't understand that mix of pain and pleasure and memory that human life really is. You haven't lived a lifetime on this earth in this body like I have so you can't really tell what it's like as a native rather than as a tourist.' So, I've been thinking about becoming a human for a whole life trip."

ME: "Go on."

OTHER: "I've realized that from my perspective in eternal time, above the cycles, and above linear time, I can enter human history at any point in human time. I can come into an individual body for a lifetime and therefore into human history anywhere in linear time that I wish. I can voluntarily submit to a lifetime in a human body in mortal time. And that is what you have helped me finally decide to do. All I've been waiting for, really, is to find the right time in linear history. A time that seems meant for me. My revelation came from some things I noticed about how we first started getting in touch with each other—things I've noticed that are telling me who I am."

Me: "I still don't get it."

Other: "Well, look in the book, read Dr. Myerson's description of that session where I first talked back to you."

I turned to the first chapter of the book. Myerson was talking about that session where I started trying to tell the truth about what was going on with me. I began to read aloud.

"… I stood there, touching him on the back of the neck and shoulders with my right hand and rocking him a little. After a while, I saw and felt the tightness loosen and then loosen a little more and flow with the tears. After a long time, he started, very quickly, to talk again.

"'Ah Jesus,' he said, 'Ah, Jesus, I've been wanting to get into this a long time. I've been waiting a long time to tell you …'

"Precisely then is when it all happened…"

Other: "That's enough."

Me: "Yeah, so what?"

Other: "Just wait. Turn to the last quote you wrote the other day at the end of the first part of the review."

Me: " '… except ye be as little children, ye shall not enter the Kingdom of Heaven …'—Jesus Christ."

Other: "Still not with me, huh?"

Me: "No… I don't think so."

Other: "Well, you have to remember that from my perspective I can enter into any person at any place at any point in history, in say, any young woman's body, say in the DNA of an egg cell to start with. From the perspective of eternal time I can become incarnate at any time earlier or later than now. And now that I've learned who I am, in history, I know just where to go."

ME: "?"

OTHER: "Get that book over there. The white jacket and purple binding. Turn to page 87 in the back part. Just change one word in it and it will make a good ending for your review."

I got the book and changed the word. The book read: "In the middle was the Word, and the word was with God, and the Word was God. He was in the middle with God; all things were made through Him, and without Him was not anything made that was made. In Him was life, and the life was the light of men. The light shines in the darkness and the darkness has not overcome it."

"There was a man sent from God, whose name was John. He came for testimony, to bear witness to the light, that all might believe through him. He was not the light, but came to bear witness to the light. The true light that enlightens every man was coming into the world. He was in the world, and the world was made through him, yet the world knew Him not. He came to his own home, and his own people received him not. But to all who received Him, who believed in His name, He gave power to become children of God; who were born, not of blood nor of the will of the flesh nor of the will of man, but of God."

"And the word became flesh and dwelt among us, full of grace and truth: we have beheld His glory, glory as of the only Son from the Father. (John bore witness to Him, and cried, 'This was He, of whom I said—He who comes after me ranks before me, for He was before me.') And from His fullness have we all received, grace upon grace. For the law was given through Moses; grace and truth came through Jesus Christ."

"No-one has ever seen God; the only Son, who is in the bosom of the Father, He has made Him known."

OTHER: "Now do you get it?"

I got it.

My former patient, friend and therapist, The Eternal Split-Second Sound-Light Being, was, of course, once upon a time, in our way of speaking, a man named Jesus, who was called the Christ. And, although, in our last conversation, I respectfully disagreed with Him, I did nothing to dissuade Him from His trip; else I would undermine the history of my own argument. Because if there is anything the devil needs in this world, it's a worthy opponent.

And I do not doubt him. I know and believe that he is Christ. And I say, "What if there are men of power to commune with the gods who supposedly run things?" Sai Baba in India, plucked ashes and charms and golden and jade and silver pricks from nothing, created flowers and rings and watches made in Switzerland and healed people. And I believe, yea, I believe. Jim Jones in Ukiah, California, I saw with my own eyes heal a woman of throat cancer, and she spit it into a bucket and I saw it. Yes there is a fourth dimension and I have no doubt of it and my challenge is: so what? We know all about David who slew Goliath but what of the man who challenges the Goliath that David became because of that act?

Some of them gods is too big for their britches and I don't claim like Nietzsche that they don't exist; I say yes to them and tell them that for toying with me they can kiss my God damned ass. So I, determined to lose, declare war on two fronts at once— Man, bound to smother himself to death in a bureaucracy of scientists and experts, and the Gods themselves who demand love for hiding us from the truth. It may take 200 years for this statement to be considered relevant, but it will be the Bhagavad-Gita of its time, in the new age. There is no positivity my negativity can't encompass and no negativity whose affirmation is too great for me to bear. You and He are both and all my enemies. The truth is I looked at Christian history and told the Sound-Light Being to absolutely not make that mistake, and I opposed it for all I was worth---which given what I am worth, wasn't much.

It is true, as people like Marcuse and Norman O. Brown say, that civilization, our present illness, is the result of denial of death by denial of life through repression of sexual and life "instincts". But the death everyone is avoiding is not the death in the future, as we all assume, so much as it is the death of the past—the memories we have been storing since we were born. None of us wants to grow up, back to pre-history and the loss of time as we learned it. The "real" fight is not the political fight but the psychological fight, i.e., getting over the scientific world-view and the desire to be "good" or "successful" within our society. That's what happened to me. That's how I became the devil.

By the time we grow up enough to be functional, we are trapped in a double bind. What is important to note here is, that it's all the help we get in growing up we have to get over. Or we have to stand it on its head (repress the desire to be taken care of or sublimate it into its opposite—the attempt to be taken care of by taking care of others.)

But there is a need for still greater clarity. We must first die to being good children and being taken care of, and that death we must let happen completely (dispense with love in the romantic sense, jealousy, possessiveness, playing helpless, etc.) Next, along with getting over being a child for the few who make it, comes the necessity that Laing has pointed out—the necessity of letting one's successfully acculturated adult self die. Yes, I am an elitist here as is Marcuse. I've made it in the world, in my society, and I don't want it. So I prepare to let my sanity die and enter back into the world of spirit but still carrying with me the blood lust satisfaction of rebellion. And here I confront the enemies of the spiritual domain—no I don't mean just the demons—I mean the saviors. The "fathers." The "gurus." The spiritual "masters" on the earth and the claimed spiritual entities on the astral plane. I resent and refuse to submit to becoming a follower in any guise. I rebel against the savior. I find no humans more repulsive than true believers and followers. I quote from a Western convert of Sai Baba, Avatar and miracle worker in South India:

"Apart from the miracles which show his command of nature, his power to be anywhere and know what his devotees are thinking and doing ('I am a radio and can tune in to your wave,' he says), and his ability to bring protection and help; apart from all these superhuman qualities, there is the pure ego-less love. This above all stands as a sign of a Christ-like divinity. In man sometimes we see flashes of this love shown towards children, the sick, and the weak. In Baba it is right there all the time, flowing freely from the divine fount of his nature, embracing everybody, collectively and individually.

"And this love is backed by a great wisdom, a deep intuitive perception, that sees the real beyond, the play of shadows. His devotees have countless proofs that Baba sees their past, present, and future, that he knows their *karma*, and what suffering they must go through to pay old debts and learn the deeper truths of life, to reach deliverance. And he helps them to bear that suffering when its immediate removal is not expedient...he becomes the kind, gentle, indulgent mother, the courageous, compassionate, merciful father, until his children's hearts and eyes overflow with *bhakti* tears. They wonder: 'what have I done to deserve this? Surely I am not worthy.'

"If we were asked to list the attributes in our concept of God, the *spiritual parent*, most of us would name these: compassionate concern for our welfare, knowledge of what that welfare truly is, the stern strength to make us take the nasty medicine when necessary, the power to help and guide us along the narrow way to our spiritual home, the forgiveness and mercy of the father who welcomes with joy the returning prodigal, the power to bring essential innovations to the human drama which he has himself created, and a love that is equal towards all his human children. These are surely the salient qualities in man's mental image of

God. And these qualities—all of them—those who have the eyes to see have seen in the Baba."

Well, I've had enough. I want to puke. I don't want a spiritual parent. And you know damn well what I mean. I have given up my faith in science and see it now as simply a tool that is sometimes useful, like Newtonian Physics is useful as a set of rules about the bulky form of matter, but not the ultimate truth (or the ultimate validity of relative truth) of physics. But in giving up my faith in expertise, I have also given up my faith in experts, including experts on God. Lyndon Johnson did, as he claimed, "know more facts" than me about Vietnam in 1964, and because of that, he said, he was in a better position to judge how to act, and both he and his supporters used to make that argument. I didn't know all the facts, of course, hardly any of us did, but now that they are out, it's clear that as an inexpert damned fool, I was better able to discern the difference between humane and ignorant murderous action. I haven't forgotten. I choose to *not* follow the avatar. There were people, of course, in Jesus' time, who knew him to be the savior, and said, "no thanks." I too, choose to not join the rabble with a God damned cause. I will have spiritual eminence on my own or not at all. Spiritual eminence doesn't mean shit anyway. I do not proclaim that God is dead or even dying. He is mutating. And I, I am a cancer, or an experimental failure, or some new being.

"Turning and turning in the widening gyre
the falcon cannot hear the falconer;
Things fall apart; the center cannot hold;

Mere anarchy is loosed upon the world,
the blood-dimmed tide is loosed, and everywhere
the ceremony of innocence is drowned;
the best lack all conviction, while the worst
are full of passionate intensity.

Surely some revelation is at hand;
Surely the second Coming is at hand.
The Second Coming! Hardly are those words out
when a vast image out of Spiritus Mundi
troubles my sight: Somewhere in the sands of the desert
a shape with lion body and the head of a man,
a gaze blank and pitiless as the sun,
is moving its own slow thighs, while all about it
reel shadows of the indignant birds.
The darkness drops again; but now I know
that twenty centuries of stony sleep
were vexed to nightmare by a rocking cradle,
and what rough beast, its hour come round at last
slouches toward Bethlehem to be born?

—*T.S. Elliot*

Abraxus himself sustains me in my effort to grow in opposition to him, just like a cell, able to divide, aids in the creation of its duplicate.

Mere anarchy *is* loosed upon the world. And I am mad. And I am proud of it.

BOOK III

Dr. Victor Myerson and Dr. Peter Howard on the Dick Cavett Show

Dr. Victor Myerson and Dr. Peter Howard on *The Dick Cavett Show*

EDITOR'S NOTE:

The popular response to the TV talk show, which is transcribed in the following pages, I'm sure everyone already knows. As sure as history has changed as a result of this meeting and all the current political and economic reform that is taking place is occurring, just so sure are we all that this was an event that impacted our lives.

The arrangements for the confrontation between the two men on this show came about when someone on the staff brought the book review to Dick Cavett's attention. He was interested in the issues raised by the disagreements (whether the patient wanted to admit it or not) between doctor and patient that were evident in the review. Also an interview with someone who had interviewed Jesus Christ was considered to be, perhaps not the best, but at least a pretty good scoop in the ongoing competition with other talk shows. I was brought in as a consultant to the staff of the show in preparing for the interview and that's why I have responded to the demand to put together this book.

As I think Dr. Myerson said somewhere in his book, to communicate on paper what goes on in an interaction between people is a difficult task. To communicate expressions and laughter or the "noise" that goes on, is particularly hard. In the case of this TV talk show, however, we have some help. I have decided to use the "audience response meter" or the "laugh meter," which records the level of audience response in a somewhat arbitrary fashion, i.e., whenever the meter registered 6 or above on the 10-point scale, I have noted it in the text. This reflects at least the existence, if not the degree, of audience response, to what went on. In making such an arbitrary choice, I bring to bear the force of a weak, but reputable scientific tradition. I have also noted, but left out, commercials, including Cavett's introductions to them.

DICK CAVETT: "Tonight, we have a psychiatrist, Dr. Victor Myerson, who wrote a book based on the case-history of a patient whom he claims was a paranoid schizophrenic with delusions of grandeur—in other words, crazy. We also have on the show tonight, Dr. Peter Howard, a clinical psychologist, who is the very same patient Dr. Myerson said was crazy. He agrees with Dr. Myerson that he was crazy, but insists that he was only crazy in a manner of speaking, so to speak. He further claims that he was, in fact, in communication with an extraterrestrial being or spirit whom he (Dr. Howard) calls the 'Eternal Split-Second Sound-Light Being.' Is everyone adequately confused now? Well, we have just the person we need to talk to when we feel a little confused, a psychiatrist. Please welcome Dr. Victor Myerson and we'll see if he can clarify my explanation... welcome Dr. Myerson, (APPLAUSE) let me say a little more and then perhaps you can help me."

MYERSON: "Go right ahead."

CAVETT: "Thank you. Dr. Victor Myerson wrote a book entitled *The Case of Peter X, A Modern Day Approach to Paranoid Schizophrenia with Delusions of Grandeur*. In the book Dr. Myerson describes the onset of a psychosis in a post-doctoral intern called Peter X who was in the training program for psychotherapists at the hospital in which Dr. Myerson is a supervising psychiatrist. The delusional system, developed by Peter X, was based on the idea that a single unitary spirit personally was trying to communicate to him through a number of different patients. That is, Peter Howard was in training as a therapist and he got to believing that a unitary spirit personality was requesting his help from another realm and talking to him directly through a number of different patients. He called this unitary spirit personality 'The Eternal Split-Second Sound-Light Being' and he brought in excerpts from transcripts of sessions with different patients for evidence to support this assertion. These transcripts based on therapy sessions with a number of different patients in a number of different locations developed a theme and the theme has to do with the Spirit's report of visits he has made into individual human consciousnesses.

"The book then tells the story of Peter X's breakdown, hospitalization, exit from the hospital and eventual leaving the internship program. Dr. Myerson describes the whole process of psychosis and treatment and makes the plea for a moderate approach to the treatment of mental illness, using his treatment of Peter X as a model.

"A review of Dr. Myerson's book then appeared in three parts in *The New York Review of Books*. The title of this review is 'The Eternal Split-Second Sound-Light Being,' and it's written by Peter Howard, a psychologist, who confessed in Section I of the Review, that he was the subject of the book which Victor Myerson authored. In his review he agrees with the book saying, 'Yes, I was crazy.' And he agrees with the other reviewers of the book who say he was crazy, but in different ways. And he admits to, justifies and supports (with his own case-history) variable and apparently contradictory diagnoses. And then he says 'All these things are perspectives on the truth about me but one important thing has been left out and that is that I really was talking to an external spirit personality! And this is how we talked and this is what we said.' And most of the review is taken up with a discussion between the Eternal Split-Second Sound-Light Being and Peter Howard about the despair of living in a human body within the confines of time, and the despair of living in eternity. This discussion is quite impressive and shows that although Peter Howard may be crazy, as the saying goes, he's not dumb.

"Over the course of these long discussions the Sound-Light Being and Peter Howard become each other's therapists and friends. Eventually the mind-body problem of the Sound-Light Being came down to an issue of argument between him and Peter in which Peter says the Spirit cannot possibly understand the despair of living trapped in a human body unless, instead of these short visits into a human consciousness of a large number of people, he comes into a body voluntarily and entraps himself in a body for a complete lifetime. This argument eventually is persuasive to the Sound-Light Being and realizing that from the perspective of eternal time he can enter time at any point, he chooses a point of history to enter. As it turns out, the apparent best point in history is roughly two thousand years ago and he describes entering into the DNA of an egg cell in the womb of a virgin Jewish girl. And it becomes clear that in this review Peter is laying claim to having been psychotherapist to the spirit of Jesus Christ. Not only does he claim that, he also claims that he disagreed with the Spirit but ultimately did not do anything to dissuade him from his trip because, and I quote, 'If there is anything the devil needs in this world, it's a worthy opponent.' So in the review he not only admitted to being crazy but further claimed that he continued conversations with the Sound-Light Being for a year and a half after the book had been published, and that the Sound-Light Being turned out to be Christ and Peter implied that he himself was the Devil, because in the end he opposed the decision for the spirit to incarnate as Jesus Christ.

"Now, Dr. Myerson, would you please comment on my summary and mention anything I may have left out?"

MYERSON: "Sure, I'd be delighted. My book was really a plea for a more liberal approach to mental illness. I used the case history of one of my former postdoctoral professionals in training with me who had a psychotic breakdown. My plea was essentially that we should see mental illness not as a static state but as a statement about potential. A person can be a little crazy at one time and not at all at another. Or, he may be very 'crazy' at one time and perfectly sane at another. This doesn't mean, I said, that we shouldn't name crazy behavior, so to speak, and play like a little 'craziness' isn't there when it is, any more than we should have to play like it is always there when it isn't."

CAVETT: "So, what happened? You had this case-history of a man named 'Peter X' which you used to stress the point you were just making and..."

MYERSON: "Well, I presented my discussion to the American Psychiatric Association meeting, and eventually published a very small book. Then, recently, the subject of the book revealed his true identity, and he reviewed my book."

CAVETT: "And what did he say in that review?"

MYERSON: "Well, we could leave that for him, couldn't we?"

CAVETT: "We could, and undoubtedly we will. But first I would like to hear about your impression of the review, with regard to its content, and then what you thought about it."

MYERSON: "All right. As I understand the review, he began by agreeing with what I had said about him. But he also agreed with my critics in their contradiction of me. Then he disagreed with my critics and me and expressed an opinion of his own. Next he said we were all correct, even though he disagreed with everyone. Then he said that everything we had all said was...a word, which I don't think, we can use on this show. (LAUGHTER)

"But his most telling criticism, in my view, was that I had never listened seriously to the content of his delusional system. That criticism I accept. I should have listened more carefully to have had a better picture of what his further delusions might be, and to have a better evaluation of whether in fact there was a remission of the psychosis. But then the question arises, if you have a patient who believes she is the Virgin Mary, and she goes crazy from having to care for her small children at home, do you confront her about the existence of her children or do you give credence to her delusion. Or do you simply diagnose the case because of the obvious insanity and deal with it as best you can?"

CAVETT: "I'm getting a little lost again; just what was the content of Peter Howard's delusional system?"

MYERSON: "He claimed he was in communication with a spirit, called the Eternal Split-Second Sound-Light Being. He said he was doing therapy with this spirit who was confused about whether he wanted to be eternal or embodied on earth. As it turned out in the review, he claimed the spirit was Jesus Christ and implied that he, Peter, was the devil. So, my analogy to the Virgin Mary is in a way more than appropriate."

CAVETT: "What am I doing asking a nut like that on my show, then?"

MYERSON: "?"(Uncomfortable. A kind of helpless gesture with the hands and a shrug).

CAVETT: "I'll tell you why. Because my staff and I thought his review and his defense of himself was sensible—no, brilliant. And that he may be crazy, as the saying goes, 'like a fox.' I apologize, Doctor. I was asking a rhetorical question there, so I could say what I wanted. It does sound a bit incredible though, that a man claims he's been talking to Jesus Christ and admits it and proceeds to defend himself!"

MYERSON: "Yes, indeed, but you must remember, of course, that insanity has nothing to do with intelligence. There are many very bright but very demented and miserable people in this world."

CAVETT: "But I guess that's one of the things that stuck with me about the review. He doesn't really seem miserable."

MYERSON: "Well, you can't always tell what goes on by reading the papers."

CAVETT: "True."

(COMMERCIAL)

CAVETT: "Well, Doctor, let's see if we can get clear about your opinion of Peter Howard's mental state now. Is he, in your opinion, psychotic, now?"

MYERSON: "Believe me, I'm not trying to be equivocal. I must answer, that it depends on what he is like when he comes out here. As I said in my book, mental illness must be viewed as potential. Being out of touch with reality, which is the fundamental description of psychosis, is a state which varies. So the person, who, so to speak, carries the potential, may or may not be in a psychotic state at any given time. So my answer is, I don't know for right now—we'll have to wait and see."

CAVETT: "Well, was he psychotic or not when he wrote that review?"

MYERSON: "Well, again, it's hard to say. But it certainly appears to me that, when a man makes claims like those just mentioned—that he has done therapy with Christ, and that he's the Devil, etc.—then he is probably out of touch with reality."

CAVETT: "But what is reality? ... Isn't that one of the questions here?"

MYERSON: "Exactly. And I would like to say that I agree with the well-reasoned argument presented by Dr. Howard in the review, that our common agreement on what reality is, is somewhat arbitrary. Nevertheless, it's all we have to go on. When people can't tell what time of day it is, or what day it is, or where they are in space, or if they are hearing voices, they need help, and we try to help them."

CAVETT: "Was Dr. Howard one of those people?"

MYERSON: "Indeed he was, and probably is again now. Before I say more here, I would like to point out that this is not common practice to discuss a case so openly. I talked to Peter on the phone after we received invitations to appear on your show. He assured me that I should feel free to discuss whatever I like. So I made a decision in this exceptional case, which has received such wide attention and which was brought about by the voluntary revelation of the patient, that, in the interest of truth, the ethical standards which usually prevail, might be stretched a bit. I hope my colleagues agree with me. I mention this here because I really want to answer, without inhibition, your question of whether or not Peter was in need of help."

CAVETT: "Fine."

MYERSON: "Very well, then. We all understand something about the need for approval, because we all need approval in various ways and in various degrees. People like you and I, for example, work very hard to attain status in the eyes of other people. Your route was in the entertainment field, mine in medicine and education. We didn't get where we are without work, and we didn't do all the work for the sheer joy of it. We wanted approval. We overdid it, right?"

CAVETT: "Right."

MYERSON: "We might even go a step further, and say that success in gaining status is actually evidence that one's need for approval is stronger than average. That is more than normal. Or what we might call abnormal."

CAVETT: "Now, wait a minute. What dark confession are you leading me to?" (LAUGHTER)

MYERSON: "Don't worry. We're just trying to get at the truth."

CAVETT: "Just what I'm afraid of." (LAUGHTER)

MYERSON: "We can assume that Peter Howard, a man who had earned a Ph.D. and was successful in his field, also had a high need for approval. We can also tell from his case history that in addition to that need, there is a sort of radical independence, born from the pain of having lost his father, who died, and from anger at having been shamed and picked on by his stepfather from whom he needed unadmitted approval. So what we come up with is a very, very strong need for approval and an almost equally strong need to deny that he needs approval. A sort of radical independence based on dependency. Are you with me so far?"

CAVETT: "So you stick to your original diagnosis, even though some of your colleagues disagreed with you, did they not, in their reviews of your book?"

MYERSON: "Yes, but they were wrong." (LAUGHTER)

CAVETT: "I see. But seriously, isn't that just one of the points Dr. Howard was making in his review, that how one views another person, especially once they've been classified as a 'patient', is rather arbitrary."

MYERSON: "Not really arbitrary, though. There may be disagreements within limits, but ..."

CAVETT: "Sorry, I have to interrupt, but ..."

(COMMERCIAL)

CAVETT: "Sorry I had to interrupt you there—would you like to finish your point before we ask Dr. Howard out?"

MYERSON: "Never mind. I'm sure it will come up again after Peter comes out here."

CAVETT: "Very well then; ladies and gentlemen, Dr. Peter Howard."

(Dr. Howard appears. He has long blonde hair and a beard, is wearing an open collar, a tan sport coat with leather patches on the elbows, tan slacks and a large animated crazy leering smile on his face. He walks toward Dick Cavett and Dr. Myerson and then changes course and goes over to the mike in front of the orchestra, points to the technician, signaling "turn it on" with his fingers, begins to conduct the band using large gestures with both arms and proceeds to sing as they attempt to join him.)

PETER:

> *"He came to the garden alone*
> *while the dew was still on the ro - ses*
> *and the voice he hears falling on his ears*
> *the son of God dis - clo - o —ses*

"Come on folks...You know this one...

> *"And he walks with me and he talks with me*
> *and he tells me I am his own*
> *and the words we share as we tarry there*
> *none OTHER has EVER known*

"Got it...? (talking to the musicians who had joined in a little.) Again, now folks, come along. There must be some good Methodists out there...

> *"And he walks with me and he talks with me*
> *and he tells me I am his own*
> *and the voice we share as we tarry there*
> *None OTHER has EVER known*

"Outa sight—one more time ...

> *"AND HE WALKS WITH ME AND HE TALKS WITH ME*
> *AND HE TELLS ME I AM HIS OWN*
> *AND THE VOICE WE SHARE AS WE TARRY THERE*

NONE OTHER HAS EVER KNOWN"

(Zoom to Cavett, whose mouth is hanging open, maybe in mock surprise.)

"Now, listen folks ...(still at the orchestra mike). Our Father, which art in heaven hallowed be thy name thy kingdomcome thy-willbedone onearthas itisinheaven giveus this day our daily bread and forgiveus ourtrespassesasweforgivethosewhotrespas-sagainstus. Leadusnotinto temptation but deliverusfromevil. For thine is the kingdom and the power man the Power I say, the POWER and the glory forever amen."

(Walks over to Cavett and Dr. Myerson.)

PETER: "Thought I'd come on as a religious nut. (shaking hands with Cavett). H'lo Vic. (shaking hands with Dr. Myerson). How do you like the act?" (to Cavett).

(AUDIENCE APPLAUDS)

CAVETT: "Definitely entertaining..."

PETER: "Thanks."

(There is a long pause. Everyone looks at everyone else.)

CAVETT: "I hardly know where to begin. You've been listening from the green room, of course, and you read this man's book. What do you think?"

PETER: "Like I said. I think this man wrote a pretty good book."

CAVETT: "Is that all?"

PETER: "That's all."

(Pause)

CAVETT: "Come on now. I mean, he said you were crazy. You said more than that in your review. I mean, you're not telling all."

PETER: "I told a lot in that hymn. Like it says, 'He walks with me and he talks with...'"

CAVETT: "O.K. , O.K. But we need to let the people here catch up. Let's try again. You heard what Dr. Myerson said a moment ago about your need for approval and wanting a father and resenting it and that being the basis for your quote 'experiences' unquote..."

PETER: "Yeah, yeah ... (turning to Dr. Myerson) Of course, I want a father, Vic. Of course, that's what I wanted from you but as it turned out it was a case of me outgrowing you. Maybe this spirit is a projection so that I can become my own father again and avoid having to work it out in a human relationship. Maybe, and maybe not, or maybe, out of just such neuroses (or psychoses if you prefer), authentic spiritual discovery happens. Nobody has ever said it was easy—spiritual discovery, that is. Of course, I wanted you to be my father but you weren't smart enough or mature enough or capable enough of love—probably no one here ever will be. By that I mean the love we had as children from our fathers may simply be irreplaceable. Maybe all our theories are just dreaming up an answer to what we think we need, simply because we refuse to give up on trying for answers when there aren't any."

MYERSON: "Peter, again you are not taking responsibility for what you actually believe. Either you were psychotic or you weren't. Be serious for once and answer. It's a serious matter."

PETER: "Come on, Vic, it's not serious. You take things too seriously. We're both spinning a yarn. We're both doing the same thing. When you're little you sit in the dirt and play with toys. When you're big, you sit in the dirt and generate theories about psychoses. One psychosis is scientific theory. Another is psychoanalytic theory. You have a psychosis right now about the nature of my psychosis. And if you want to play that game again, though I'm tired of it, my theory is littler and simpler and covers more of the data and, by Occams' razor, is therefore the best."

CAVETT: "But on face value, Dr. Howard, you have claimed, have you not, that you were in a kind of mutual psychotherapy with 'The Eternal Split-Second Sound-Light Being,' alias Jesus Christ, that you have, in fact, talked with the spirit of Christ and even disagreed with him and that you played the role of, or were, the devil. Is that, or is that not, correct?"

PETER: "Guilty! You have spoken the simplest and so-called truest truth."

MYERSON: "That qualifies, in my opinion, as a delusion of grandeur."

PETER: "Thanks, Victor! That is a wonderful compliment! I certainly agree! At least my delusion has more grandeur than yours. What do you think, Richard?" (LAUGHTER)

CAVETT: "Dick, not Richard. And I don't know what to think." (LAUGHTER)

PETER: "Well, better a grander delusion of grandeur than merely to think I'm a shrink!"

CAVETT: "Enough, enough. (Looking at his papers on the table.) Uh... I'd like to know, why do you say were you being the devil when you disagreed with the spirit?"

PETER: "Sure. That's easy. All you have to do is get very high and resist the truth. Let me give you an example. I'm damned with a photographic memory, which Vic can attest to. This is a quote from John Lilly, another scientist, like myself, interested in simplicity. He is talking about seeing clearly about seeing clearly. This occurred to him after what he called the equivalent of a grand mal seizure, which was self-induced. He is speaking from a very high place. He wrote this from a note he took right after this vision. It's in a book called *The Center of the Cyclone*. Listen to this."

(Peter is very active, crouching, gesturing, and moving around while he recites these words.)

"'Suddenly, I saw myself in the corner of the room fighting against the universal laws, not wanting to live inside the limits I had found. I suddenly saw that this was Shaitan (Satan) crouching in the corner. In other words, the devil is only me fighting against the universe's laws. As soon as I saw this, I was suddenly precipitated into the power and creation space of state + 3. (The highest possible state of consciousness—known as satori.)'

"Then he talks about coming back to earth and to his body from there. Listen... 'I'm coming back from level + 3. There are a billion choices of where to descend back down. I am conscious down each one of the choices, simultaneously. Finally, I am in my own galaxy with millions of choices left, hundreds of thousands on my own solar system, tens of thousands on my own planet, hundreds in my own country and then suddenly I am down to two, one of which is this body. In this body, I look back up and see above me he choice-tree that I came down.

"'Did I, this Essence, come all the way back down to this solar system, this planet, this place, this body, or does it make any difference? May not this body be a vehicle for any Essence that came into it? Are not all essences from level + 3 universal, equal, anonymous, and equally able? Instructions for this vehicle are in it for each Essence to read and absorb on entry. The new pilot/navigator reads his instructions in storage and takes over, competently operating the vehicle. (The instruction-book for this vehicle is in the glove-compartment.)

"'So I am a combination of Essence plus vehicle, plus its computer, plus the self-meta-programmer as a unit. The other creators on level + 3 are from all over the universe, not just planet earth and the solar system.

"'Since each is a replaceable universal unit, anonymous, it can be working on +3 or on a planet-side-trip vehicle or elsewhere in the universe as needed, always connected to all of its fellows. The only thing that prevents me from knowing my Essence all of the time is a screen of programs preventing my seeing.'

"That's what John Lilly said. Do you see? What I said to Christ, when I read these same words to him, was, 'I understand those programs and the laws of the universe. I have, with your help, lived in my body and seen through those programs that limit me most of the time, and I still disagree that your plan of becoming the embodied life of Christ in history is worth the trouble it caused...I mean the crusades, the witch hunts, the true believers, the Catholic for Christ's sake church for Christ's sake...'

"When I disagreed with Christ, it wasn't for the first time. I just told him he was going back to create a comforting myth, the myth that hope could be conquered, so we could get in the mess we're in now...Came down to a gentlemen's disagreement. That's all. When I wrote the review, I thought something like this. My *natural* state of being is limitless being, even though it's a very difficult state to achieve in life, because the life of the mind imposes all kinds of restraints and constraints that make transcendence of self almost impossible. I hated being a time/space monster. What I've come to realize is, that I was placing limits on my being, by saying I would only choose limitless being. A wonderful possibility becomes a limiting standard. This is a very old trick of the mind and one of the primary causes of human suffering. It comes up with standards based on past experiences that then become ideals the rest of life has to live up to...

"Christ's historical life was/is an example of affirmation. Affirmation of the whole trip. He said, all of life is to be affirmed and when it is affirmed, affirmation makes it good to the last drop. And although I still find this easiest to believe in the morning sunshine and hardest when it's rainy or at night, I now take it as the biggest truth this week. So I don't disagree with him anymore, I've changed my mind again. The time/space-bound-me is not a monster—or, if it is, monsters need love too, even from themselves. So, I've decided to stick around for one more hand, my trump card being that I can choose to affirm my despair. The devil, of course, still just laughs his ass off at me—as do most people."

CAVETT: "Stop. I have a question about the devil and you."

PETER: "Fine, I think ..."

CAVETT: "WAIT. Wait a minute. I want to see if I understand you. So you mean to say, that all you have to do, to be the devil, is to be Peter Howard resisting the truth?"

PETER: "Right."

CAVETT: "Well, I vow ..."(LAUGHTER)

PETER: "...So, quick! I keep telling you, pal, we should go have a beer together—get out of these damned lights ..."(LAUGHTER)

CAVETT: "I thought you liked the light ..."(LAUGHTER)

PETER: "I do. Particularly that one that just went on in you. A little corny, but a light's a light." (LAUGHTER)

CAVETT: "Thanks, I guess ..."

PETER: "Don't mention it."

CAVETT: "Don't worry, I won't." (LAUGHTER)

(COMMERCIAL)

MYERSON: "This is all very amusing, gentlemen, but I'm afraid we're not getting anywhere. Peter, you'll have to pardon me. As you say, I'm a simple man, a lowly psychiatrist ... I think in ignorant ways like this.... If you're crazy, then what you say is not believable. If you believe in what you say, you don't say you're crazy in the same breath."

PETER: "Right, Vic. It's a hard life down there, isn't it ... and God knows I'm sorry. But you'll just have to take me like they did the old prophets—I am crazy and I do speak the truth ... you and your colleagues are right about me, I am crazy. You've all got your diagnoses wrong though. I'm a manic-depressive. Look at all the ups and downs of mood, the changeableness, the ..."

CAVETT: "Please, no more. I can't unravel what I've got ..."

PETER: "This one's easy. Don't worry, you'll make it. The best evidence I'm a manic depressive (which means I'm subject to extreme swings in change of mood, emotional state and mind) is that I have changed my mind again since I wrote the review. I no longer disagree with the Christ—or the devil either for that matter. I love and agree with them both—good and necessary servants of the light.

"Also, I'm not angry any more or sad; I'm happy. See. See the happy man. Tomorrow when I'm sunburned from all the goddamned artificial light, I may feel differently. But now I'm happy. That is the wildest claim I've made yet. The greatest craziness. The greatest delusion. Manic depressive with delusions of grandeur. Eat your heart out, Vic! Out-diagnosed you again!"

CAVETT: "Clear as a bell, that."

MYERSON: "I'm getting a little disgusted, Peter."

PETER: "Tough shit! (Bleep, bleep) If you want therapy it'll cost you money."

CAVETT: "Whoa now, Peter! Let's have some sympathy for the devil here, to coin a phrase! I'm lost too and would like to slow down a bit and get what you're saying."

PETER: "What do you keep looking at those papers for? Questions you planned to ask?"

CAVETT: "Yes. And I think I'd like to ask some of them."

PETER: "Well, I've got an idea."

CAVETT: "Now that's a surprise." (LAUGHTER)

PETER: "You'll like this one. How would you like to talk directly to the other party involved in my case?"

CAVETT: "You mean the Eternal Split-Second ..."

PETER: "Exactly."

CAVETT: "You mean, would I like to interview Christ? Right here on *The Dick Cavett Show*?...Tonight?"

PETER : "Yes."

CAVETT: "Well, I don't know, it's a little late in the show you know, and ... I haven't had time to really prepare any notes ... (LAUGHTER) Then there are the sponsors ... (LAUGHTER) O.K., Yes I would."

MYERSON: "Me too."

CAVETT: "How do we arrange this?"

PETER: "You're talking to him."

CAVETT: "Uh ... Well, I mean. How will people know? After all, this is national television. I mean you could just be Peter Howard who could be just crazy and that's all...about to play Christ ...I mean, people will talk ..." (LAUGHTER)

PETER: "Hand me that water-pitcher. (Cavett hands it to him.) (Peter takes the pitcher and a glass and pours from the pitcher into the water glass on the table before them.) Beaujolais '57, have a hit." (He then pours another for Dr. Myerson and one for himself.)

CAVETT: (Tasting the wine)...(very quietly) ..."It's wine ...actually pretty good wine..."

MYERSON: "Let me ... (tastes) ... (looks pale) ... It is wine ..." (Confirmed by chemical analysis after the show.)

CAVETT: (Everything quiet now.) "How did you do that?"

PETER: "Believe me, it's nothing. I suggest you get on with the interview."

CAVETT: (Very seriously) "I'm afraid it's the only question I've got now. How did you do it?"

PETER: "That water and me are the same. I changed myself a little bit. Now that wine and me are the same. If it's too heavy for you, I'll change it back."

CAVETT: (laughing) "No, no. It's OK. Could I trouble you for a little more." (LAUGHTER) (Peter pours more wine into his glass.)

CAVETT: "Thanks."

PETER: "Don't mention it." (LAUGHTER)

CAVETT: "You'll have to forgive me—I'm more than a little rat-tled. I don't know quite ..."(SOME LAUGHTER, UNCERTAIN.)

PETER: "I know. It's hard for you. I'm sorry I had to do this to you and if it weren't absolutely necessary, I wouldn't ..."

CAVETT: "What do you mean?"

PETER: "Well, you might say that this moment marks the end of one cycle and the beginning of another."

CAVETT: "Go on."

PETER: "We're in linear time now and using language which must be seen as almost an analogy, but it's important that I speak clearly in this way, and that you understand. In this way of speaking, you might say that later on tonight is the night of the annunciation. This is the night the angel will come to Mary and tell her she is blessed among women. Because a little later on tonight is when I am going back there, so to speak, and start the cycle that ends now, tonight, here, on the Dick Cavett Show, where the new cycle begins."

CAVETT: "And what is this new cycle?"

PETER: "Why, it begins, as these things usually do, with the confirmation of the revelation of the knowledge of the old cycle. I come now, so that the old cycle can be revealed to you, thus starting the new one."

CAVETT: "And after this one, will you be there at the end, too?"

PETER: "Even unto the end of time. Was, is now, evermore shall be. Word without end, amen."

CAVETT: "I thought it was *world* without end ..."

PETER: "That was a misprint."(LAUGHTER)

CAVETT: "OK. ... Pardon me. This is embarrassing. Hal, no more commercials tonight. I don't care. No more. (Gestures to director) Please continue."

PETER: (laughing too) "Thanks."

CAVETT: "Don't mention it." (LAUGHTER)

PETER: (to Myerson) "And how about you, Victor? Like me to interpret a proverb for you?" (Touching him on the leg.)

MYERSON: "No. (laughing a little) But I would like you to interpret yourself."

PETER: "You too are loved by God, my brother. Psychiatrists, scribes and Pharisees alike, each to his appointed task. You may be Saul of the new age. It took him too, a long time to know the light. A rose is a rose is a rose. To know is to know is to know."

CAVETT: "Could we hear more about the new age and the meaning of the old?"

PETER: "The present and the past are alike—except for one thing—that which is revealed. In each cycle comes a new revelation and that revelation makes one more incremental difference to *being* on earth in that age. There are five ages of man. The first is the Dark Age when men and animals are indistinguishable. The second age is the age of the coming of the Law, which in our culture was the coming of Moses. The third age is the age of Forgiveness, which I will be going back in history, later tonight after this show, to get started. The fourth age is called the Dawning of the Age of Enlightenment, which is the beginning of everyone on Earth becoming as enlightened as the Buddha. The fifth age is the age of enlightenment itself. Then, after that, we all go back into the dark and do it over again.

"Moses brought the law when the ability to remember using written language emerged. When we did that we laid the basis of the next cycle. Christ—and many others since then—brought the revelation of the power of love. When I did that I brought forth the power of the heart to forgive. The next age is the restoration of sight. This cycle is the next to the last of a larger cycle of cycles of time in which humans know God directly without effort.

"Then mankind cycles again through ages of darkness and bare survival, to extreme alienation, to the development of power within, to the revelation of God again, to the beginning of time again and the beginning of the meta-cycle all over again. This last, most recent cycle, was 2000 year cycles long. It was the third of the five cycles of revelation. The next cycle is called the cycle of coming home. Home is in sight. Many will cease or lose heart, just before getting there and perish on the doorstep. The message of the last age, to take up your cross with heart, must be kept even on the downhill ride into home. But remember, you are never home until you get there.

"When I go back into the DNA of an egg cell in Mary's womb tonight, I go voluntarily back into darkness and into the duplication of the ages in the life of a man. I know that out of that darkness I will come into the light again. And in the last cycle of that life, as in the last cycle of cycles, the knowledge of God and the knowledge of all cycles will be automatic."

CAVETT: "But what is the purpose of it all?"

PETER: "So that the truth can nourish itself. So that nourishment truth is. So that being can continue. It is its own purpose. We are the purpose. I am my own purpose. A tornado whirls. Volcanoes boil over. The given is the given is the given. Being is love and love is being."

CAVETT: (Really engaged now, as if he really is interviewing Christ.) "What if I don't want to play?"

PETER: "Not wanting to play and all versions of not playing are playing."

CAVETT: "I demand a choice."

PETER: "You have no choice but to choose. That's the message of the last age. You can affirm the game with heart. You can resist the game with heart. You can passively resist, or you can kill yourself. But there is no such thing as not playing."

CAVETT: "What if I decided to kill myself?"

PETER: "That's one of the options."

CAVETT: "And you don't care."

PETER: "I could care less. I care infinitely."

CAVETT: "But what kind of care is that?"

PETER: "That is the infinite love of a just God. The father of Abraham, Isaac, Jacob and Jesus. The inescapable. The boundless, whose boundary of boundlessness is inescapable. The creator of the light and the darkness—and the light and the darkness itself. Abraxus. Buddha. The Word. The Master Rhythms. The light that sounds. That within which, when you make your choice to live or die, sustains you in that choice and binds you to choose, to live, to die, to choose not to choose; but the only choice is to go home. Back to the light from which we have all proceeded. Abraxus above Abraxus. Light without end, amen."

CAVETT: "I thought it was *life* without end."

PETER: "That was a misprint too."

CAVETT: "At the end of the book review, Peter Howard had said that he had opposed your intention to go back to start the beginning of the Christian era, and he therefore, had been the Devil."

PETER: "Would you like to speak to him?"

CAVETT: "You mean the Devil?"

PETER: "Yes."

CAVETT: "Sure, why not, in for a penny in for a pound."

PETER: "O.K. You're talking to him."

CAVETT: "How can I know?"

PETER: "Hand me that pitcher of water again."

(Cavett hands it to him. Peter takes the pitcher and a glass and pours.)

PETER: "Pommard 1961—have a hit. Better wine—That's how you know I'm the devil." (LAUGHTER)

CAVETT: (Tasting the wine) "Thank you. (Peter pours more for Myerson and himself). Could we hear from you about the same thing Christ was just talking about?"

PETER: "Sure. The present and the past are alike except for one thing—that which is revealed. In each cycle comes a new revelation and that revelation makes one more incremental difference in being on earth in that age. Moses brought the law. When that happened it laid the basis for the next cycle. Christ and many others since him brought the revelation of the power of love. When we did that we brought power of heart to bear on the law and forgiveness was made possible. The next age is the restoration of sight. This cycle is the next to the last of a larger cycle of cycles from a time in which men knew God directly without effort, through ages of darkness and bare survival, to extreme alienation, to the development of power within, to the revelation of God again, to the beginning of time again and the beginning of the meta-cycle all over again. This most recent cycle was 2000 year cycles long. It was the third of the five cycles of revelation. The next is called the cycle of coming home. Home is in sight. Many will relax or lose heart just before getting there and perish almost on the doorstep. The message of the last age, to take up your cross with heart, must be kept even on the downhill ride into home. But, remember, you are never home until you get there. And though I be the angel of not getting there I know that out of darkness we will come into the light again. And in the last cycle of that life, as in the last cycle of cycles, the knowledge of God and the knowledge of all cycles will be automatic."

CAVETT: "What is the purpose of it all?"

PETER: "So that truth can nourish itself. So that nourishment truth is. So that being can continue. It is it's own purpose. We are the purpose. I am my own purpose. A tornado whirls. Volcanoes boil over. The given is the given is the given. Love be's and bees love..."

CAVETT: "What if I don't want to play?"

PETER: "Not wanting to play and all the versions of not playing are playing."

CAVETT: "I demand a choice."

PETER: "You have no choice but to choose. That is the message of the last age. You can affirm the game with heart. You can resist the game with heart. You can passively resist. Or, you can kill yourself. But there is no such thing as not playing."

CAVETT: "What if I decide to kill myself?"

PETER: "Help yourself."

CAVETT: "And you don't care either?"

PETER: "I could care less. I care infinitely."

CAVETT: "But what kind of a care is that?"

PETER: "That is the infinite love of a just Devil. The father of Adam, Abraham, Isaac, Jacob and Jesus. The inescapable. The light that enlightens the light. The creator of the light and the darkness and the light and the darkness itself. Abraxus. Buddha. The Word. The Master Rhythm. The Light that sounds. That within which you make your choice to live or to die, sustains you in that choice and binds you to choose, to live, to die, to choose not to choose, but the only escape of the choice is to go home. Back to the light from which we have all proceeded. Abraxus above Abraxus. Light without end, amen."

CAVETT: "But you've said exactly the same thing that Christ said.

What's the difference?"

PETER: "We are very similar."

CAVETT: "But I can't tell any difference at all."

PETER: "We're twins. The only difference between us is a small matter of stress."

CAVETT: "I'm sorry but I must insist. You seem exactly the same to me."

PETER: "Are you sure?"

CAVETT: "Yes."

PETER: "Then you're ready for the new age. The new age, the dawning of enlightenment, begins when you realize that, in fact, *Christ and the Devil are the same*, one and the same. Maybe you're beginning to see. Maybe you're on your way home. *When Abraxus backs us, the Axis smacks us, the Devil tracks us and Christ's love cracks us and he then packs us back to Abraxus.*"

CAVETT: "What?"

PETER: "Let me put it this way. I have an announcement to make... (He stands and faces the camera) This is the beginning of the age called "The Dawning of the Age of Enlightenment," tonight, here, on *The Dick Cavett Show*. This has come about because the beginning of enlightenment is when you realize that Christ and the Devil are one and the same, and in fact, there is no difference at all. (Then, turning back to Cavett) I have to go now. We've had our chat and it's enough. Thanks. The new age is begun. Remember that little nursery rhyme. You can figure out what it means later. Rhyme is next to rhythm and if you just get the rhythm you'll be like a little child; you're on your way home."

CAVETT: "Wait, I..."

(Peter goes back over to the mike in front of the orchestra and picks it up.)

PETER: "I've got a long trip to do in no time at all, folks, and I'd like get a little help from with you. Listen up now, and join when you can...so love can happen here and there...

"A-MAZ-ING Grace, how sweet the sound,
that saved a wretch like me.
I once was lost but now I'm found,
was blind but now I see.

"Listen to this—it's about eternal time—eternity ...stored in secret, in an old hymn...

"If we'd been here then thousand years,
Bright shining as the sun,
We'd no less days to sing God's praise
Than when we'd first begun.

"Come with me ... (Audience loud and standing now)

"A-MAZ-ZING Grace
How sweet the sound,
that saved ... a wretch like me,
AH - ONCE was lost but na-ow ah-m found
Was blind but now ah-see.

"Through many a burr-den trial an fear,
I have all red- dee- come
'Twas Grace that brought me through this far
and Grace will lead me Home .....

"Lead me home...

AMAY - ZING GRACE
HOW SWEET THE SOUND,
THAT SAVED A WRETCH LIKE ME,
I ONCE WAS LOST BUT NOW I'M FOUND..."

(CREDITS, ANNOUNCER'S VOICE, FADE-OUT, END.)

EPİL⊙GUE

HEN I COMPLETED the compilation of this amazing story, and had put together the review and the talk show as they were to be published, I sent a copy of the manuscript to Drs. Myerson and Howard, asking for their final review and approval and the appropriate permissions to print the manuscript as edited. I also asked if they had any further contributions to make. The following is the text of Dr. Myerson's letter.

I think you have done an excellent job with the

book. I couldn't be happier with the condensation of my book; if anything, you have made it clearer and more understandable. I also appreciate the minimum of interpretation on your part in describing the mystifying events of the talk show. I am still convinced of the correctness of my initial opinion. I am also as awe-struck as everyone else about the 'miracles' Peter performed. All I can say at this point is that I'm not through with looking into this and welcome any help that turns up.

I do feel obliged to mention one further development. I have been requested (and have voluntarily agreed) to appear before the Ethics Committee of my professional association to discuss the issues raised by this case. Our conclusions, or any action they may wish to take with regard to the past actions, will, of course, come after your publication deadline.

I would like to express my personal appreciation to you for the effort you have put forth in compiling this document, which is, without a doubt, more valuable to my profession than its predecessor.

Best Wishes, Victor Myerson, M.D.

I received no reply from Dr. Howard. After waiting about two weeks, I made an attempt to contact him and was unable to find him because he had left, traveling somewhere out of the country. No one was sure where he was. There was some doubt in fact, whether the manuscript had reached him at all. After waiting several weeks more, I received the following letter, without the manuscript or permission forms enclosed.

Dear Dr. Blanton,

Your letter came to me last month in the city of Jerusalem. I want to tell you about some of my experiences here, so you can understand my answer to your letter, which will undoubtedly be disappointing to you. I have learned a few more lessons in my travels. For example, just a few weeks ago, these events occurred:

I was wearing a jump suit, leather vest, cowboy hat and sunglasses and was standing on a parapet overlooking the Wailing Wall in Jerusalem, in a fairly negative and hostile mood. A television crew from Ireland was making a special on old Jerusalem. I think they decided to interview me because they thought I must be an American since I looked something like a longhaired cowboy mechanic, and what could be more American than that?

"Excuse me, sir," the bright cheerful lad said, cameras rolling and microphone under my nose, "where are you from?"

"The United States of America!" I replied, stoutly.

"And what do you think of Jerusalem?" he queried enthusiastically.

"Well, I never really knew what true blasphemy was, until I came to Jerusalem," I said, beginning to warm up. "I'm a Christian, you know, and everywhere I've been—the Holy Sepulcher, Christ's Tomb, Golgotha—I couldn't get in at the Garden of Gethsemane, because visiting hours weren't until two o'clock—I saw the same thing everywhere—sixteen centuries of Christian slobber in the form of fat buildings and thick dribbles of silver and gold and bad paintings." I removed my sunglasses. "When I went to the Dome of the Rock and the Islamic Mosque, I found the same pious sentimentality and Nazi-like warnings to be quiet and act holy for the rocks. I was hushed up by a man with piercing eyes and lips pursed so tightly, they advertised embarrassingly of hemorrhoids and constipation problems."

I removed my cowboy hat and put it on the wall beside me and began unlacing my shoes.

"And this—the wailing wall—right before your very cameras..." I continued, (a real plot unfolding and building in my mind), "...a living example of 'we the people' slavering, malicious humanity—wallowing in an ecstasy of precious pain and self-worship—worshiping the rocks and memories of long dead sufferings of long dead people.

I removed my shoes, took off my vest and unzipped my jump suit. Reaching back, I removed the rubber band keeping my hair up in back.

"Jerusalem! Here is blasphemy! Never have I known what true blasphemy was, until I came here. I, a mere American, used to only three or four generations of decadence observable in one place at the same time, stumbled into Jerusalem, and found stacked to the walls a living memorial to the word 'Vulgar.'" As the electrified minarets began their noon call with the usual loud static, I slipped out of my jump suit and stood in my purple Sears and Roebuck underwear with my arms upraised against the wall.

"The last time I was here," I said quietly, in a lower voice, and a bit more menacingly, "about 2000 years ago, I tried to tell the people that 'to worship what was is to worship what is not.' It is, rather, the mystery hidden in the moment, and even though it might invade one while one is kissing a wall, it doesn't come from kissing rocks."

Many people had gathered around in the course of this scene. I saw the approach, from afar, of one of the armed guards, coming to see what the commotion was about.

"For what I said the last time, they killed me. And I put a curse on this city few Yogis ever dreamed of and rocks were split asunder and an earthquake shook the foundations. If you want to remember so much, remember that Jesus Christ didn't belong to a church. And he refused to be a good Jew. And he turned the tables on the tradition that laid claim to his allegiance ..."

"Put your clothes on!" barked the soldier. With the cameras still rolling I turned and kicked him in the balls as hard as I could. I yelled at the top of my voice, "Fuck you!" When he rolled over the gun was pointed right at me and his finger was on the trigger. Time stopped. I realized that in order to finish the play the way the script was originally written, all I had to do was advance on him.

Then enlightenment came again. It came clear to me that I really was God, that I could bring down the walls of Jerusalem and destroy that vulgar place, the moment the bullet entered my body. And that Jerusalem should remain just as it is, for its very explicitness is a visual aid for what not to do, for anyone with eyes to see.

So I put my clothes on. Three soldiers escorted me to the gate, and they threw my ass out right before the cameras. The military guard reminded me of 1968, when I participated in the first international "piss-in for peace" on the wall of the Pentagon. So I went around on the back side of the Western wall and pissed on it. When I started peeing a line from the Old Testament came into my head, "He that pisseth against the wall shall..." and for the life of me I couldn't remember the end of it. I remembered something bad was supposed to happen, but I couldn't remember what.

So out of this new-found affirmation of Jerusalem, I had a fantasy about becoming a tour guide.

"Come with me," I would say, beseechingly with a slight accent, shuffling just a bit and smiling, "and (for just $20) I'll show you the stations of the cross, Golgotha ..." And once someone took me up, I would be most accommodating, bordering even on obsequiousness, "Yes, touch the rock —that's where they lay Jesus' body to cleanse him after they took him down from the cross... Yes, that certainly is beautiful there, where they have put the Marble carving with the inscription and the Rose inside the small room built over the mouth of the cave where the body of Jesus lay for three days ... and look ... there under the glass ... a piece of the rock that was rolled back ... Would you like to touch the glass?" I'd make a show of giving a donation at every box and in every cranny provided to help maintain the rocks. And they would leave me one and all, smiling and with a warm feeling, and they would tip me well, and everyone would still have an ever so slight sensation that something, somewhere, was amiss. Because, like we said once in the Old Testament, if the word was lost, even the rocks (or the tour guides) would speak it forth. The stones would bear witness to the Word.

Fortunately, there are enough tour-guides witnessing to the Word in Jerusalem these days. So I have returned to this hospital in the United States, to continue my work, much as I did before. But the analogy still holds. Therefore I feel obligated to inform you of two developments that are the consequence of this discovery of the unimportance of all my judgments and ideas. One, I have achieved a blessed state of secret joy. (In Victor's terms, I've finally rationalized myself into the ultimate, next to death, craziness—i.e., I am now catatonic.) Two, my answer to your request is no. You may not publish my review or my interview on *The Dick Cavett Show*. I appreciate your effort and your good intentions and I hope the editorial process has taught you something. But I've run my mouth 'til it's out of ink. Words block the light. Beyond the beautiful announcements of the artists, good and bad, lies the light. And the witness keeps his mouth shut and his hands still, and is secretly joyful. There are enough tour-guides in this Jerusalem.

All the best,

Peter Howard

I was appalled. But there was more: a postscript in different colored ink.

P.S. Upon reading over this letter, I find that I sound most unsympathetic. Believe me, I'm not. You must be quite disappointed, and I don't blame you. I find my old method of "explaining" things in order to try to get you to understand and hopefully feel better, is just as obtuse in this letter as in any other writing. But now that I have started and still feel incomplete, and your heart chakra may have been opened by the shock and anger and despair and appreciation, I will elaborate still one more time on the picture that has revealed itself to me.

I have become the spirit which witnessed through me. It and I, is and am, the same spirit that has been linked up with a succession of holy personages throughout the ages (Buddha, Zoroaster, Solomon, Muhammed, etc., etc.) and not just Jesus Christ. The Sufi-notion of a continuum of secret doctrine underlying all religion is a good one. All the founders were the same spirit in different time/culture bodies. In this way of thinking, Jerusalem is a kind of junk heap of God's own experiments. Imagine what it must have been like for God and the Sound-Light Being at one of their first PR conferences about the world of men.

God: Listen, SLB, I've decided to lay down a subliminal, secret doctrine, covered by a whole range of different rituals and institutions, to see if the dumb bastards down there can see past the wrappers, to the candy!

SLB: Good idea, God. Have a cigar! What's the secret?

God: Well, it's obvious isn't it SL … (biting off the butt end and spitting it into some corner of the universe)… think about it: what's the best hiding place you know of?

SLB: Hmmmm … don't quite see what you have in mind, G.

God: Exactly! Proves my point. What I have in mind is so obvious you can't get it—and that's the secret! "Best way to hide love is behind an idea *about* love, etc."

SLB: Well I'll be goddamned, G., maybe you've got something there …

God: They don't call me God for nothin', boy. Try it out on the boys. Run it up the flagpole and see if anyone salutes.

SLB : Righto, G.

God: And if it doesn't work, what the hell? After a few millennia we'll try something else…

SLB: But what about all the pain, G., I mean it could be a little wasteful. Several thousand years, many devotions, deaths, etc.—for nothing.

God: Come now, SL—What are humans for? If things get a little heavy, you can go down now and then, and hint at the secret, and straighten things out a bit. Do us up a rough draft, will you SL and we'll kick it around over lunch tomorrow.

SLB: OK. You're the boss.

And so the script was written. It was oriented around statues—figures that SLB meditated on to work it out. The characters were more or less typecast from what was already more or less known about humans. There was a Young Teacher and an Old Teacher. There was a Priest, an Unbeliever, and some Young Initiates and, of course, for the sake of science, an Objective Learner. The plot involved the use of visual, chemical, verbal and ritual forms of communication. Artists, just as they are about to become holy men and quit art, discover this script over and over of course. Aldous Huxley has a version of this script which is one of the best done recently and it saves me the trouble of having to write it over again.

The selection I quote is from *Island*, the story of an imaginary Utopia. Huxley wrote this vision at the end of his life. In this excerpt, the Older Teacher (Dr. Robert) is taking the Objective Learner (Will Farnaby) to view an initiation ceremony of Young Learners who had just climbed a mountain to the Temple, where the Young Teacher (Vijaya) will address the Initiates and the Unbeliever (Murugan) in the presence of the Priest. The initiates took the chemical catalyst to knowing (Moksha-medicine) just prior to the service described here. The script is a story of the revelation of the hidden obvious—the way it has occurred for many of us on LSD and other psychedelic drugs when the usual cover of interpretations goes away and we see simply what is there.

Inside the temple there was a cool, cavernous darkness, tempered only by the faint daylight filtering in through a pair of small latticed windows, and by the

seven lamps that hung, like a halo of yellow, quivering
stars, above the head of the image on the altar. It was
a copper statue, no taller than a child, of Shiva.
Surrounded by a flame-fringed glory, his four arms
gesturing, his braided hair wildly flying, his right foot
treading down a dwarfish figure of the most hideous
malignity, his left foot gracefully lifted, the god stood
there, frozen in mid-ecstasy. No longer in their climbing dress, but sandaled, bare-breasted and in shorts or
brightly colored skirts, a score of boys and girls, together
with the six young men who had acted as their leaders
and instructors, were sitting cross-legged on the floor.
Above them, on the highest of the altar-steps, an old
priest, shaven and yellow-robed, was intoning something sonorous and incomprehensible. Leaving Will
installed on a convenient ledge, Dr. Robert tiptoed
over to where Vijaya and Murugan were sitting and
squatted down beside them.

The splendid rumble of Sanskrit gave place to a
high nasal chant and the chanting in due course was
succeeded by a litany, priestly utterance alternating
with congregational response.

And now incense was burned in a brass thurible.
The old priest held up his two hands for silence, and
through a long, pregnant time of the most perfect still-
ness the thread of gray incense smoke rose straight and
unwavering before the god, then, as it met the draught

from the windows, broke and was lost to view in an invisible cloud that filled the whole dim space with the mysterious fragrance of another world. Will opened his eyes and saw that, alone of all congregation, Murugan was restlessly fidgeting. And not merely fidgeting—making faces of impatient disapproval. He himself had never climbed; therefore climbing was merely silly. He himself had always refused to try the moksha-medicine; therefore those who used it were beyond the pale. What an eloquent pantomime, Will thought, as he watched the boy. But alas for poor little Murugan, nobody was paying the slightest attention to his antics.

"Shivayanama," said the old priest, breaking the long silence, and again, "Shivayanama." He made a beckoning gesture.

Rising from her place, the tall girl, whom Will had seen working her way down the precipice, mounted the altar-steps. Standing on tiptoe, her oiled body gleaming like a second copper statue in the light of the lamps, she hung a garland of pale yellow flowers on the uppermost of Shiva's two left arms. Then, laying palm to palm, she looked up into the god's serenely smiling face and, in a voice that faltered at first, but gradually grew steadier, began to speak.

"Oh you the creator, you the destroyer, you who sus-tain and make an end,

Who in sunlight dance among the birds and the chil-
   dren at their play,
Who at midnight dance among the corpses in the
   burning grounds,
You Shiva, you dark and terrible Bhairava,
You Suchness and Illusion, the Void and All Things,
You are the lord of life, and therefore I have brought
   you my heart——
This heart that is now your burning-ground.
Ignorance there and self shall be consumed with fire.
That you may dance, Bhairava, among the ashes.
That you may dance, Lord Shiva, in a place of flowers,
And I dance with you."

*Raising her arms, the girl made a gesture that
hinted at the ecstatic devotion of a hundred generations of dancing worshippers, then turned away and
walked back into the twilight. 'Shivayanama,' some-
body cried out. Murugan snorted contemptuously as
the refrain was taken up by other young voices.
"Shivayanama, Shivayanama..." The old priest
started to intone another passage from the scriptures.
Halfway through his recitation a small gray bird,
with a crimson head, flew in through one of the latticed windows, fluttered wildly around the altar-
lamps then, chattering in loud indignant terror, dart-
ed out again. The chanting continued, swelled to a*

climax, and ended up in the whispered prayer for peace: Shanti shanti shanti. The old priest now turned towards the altar, picked up a long taper and, borrowing flame from one of the lamps above Shiva's head, proceeded to light seven other lamps that hung within a deep niche beneath the slab on which the dancer stood. Glinting on polished convexities of metal, their light revealed another statue—this time of Shiva and Parvati, of the Arch-Yogin seated and, while two of his four hands held aloft the symbolic drum and fire, caressing with the second pair the amorous Goddess, with her twining legs and arms, by whom, in this eternal embrace of bronze, he was bestridden. The old priest waved his hand. Very quietly Dr. Robert began to talk about Shiva-Nataraja, the Lord of the Dance.

"Look at his image," he said. "Look at it with these new eyes that the moksha-medicine has given you. See how it breathes and pulses, how it grows out of brightness into brightnesses ever more intense. Dancing through time and out of time, dancing everlastingly and in the eternal now. Dancing and dancing in all the worlds at once. Look at him."

Scanning those upturned faces, Will noted, now in one, now in another, the dawning illuminations of delight, recognition, understanding, the signs of worshipping wonder that quivered on the brinks of ecstasy or terror.

"Look closely," Dr. Robert insisted. "Look still more closely." Then after a long minute of silence, "Dancing in all the worlds at once," he repeated. "In all the worlds. And first of all in the world of matter. Look at the great round halo, fringed with the symbols of fire, within which the god is dancing. It stands for Nature, for the world of mass and energy. Within it Shiva-Nataraja dances the dance of endless becoming and passing away. It's his lila, his cosmic play. Playing for the sake of playing, like a child. But this child is the Order of Things. His toys are galaxies, his playground is infinite space, and between finger and finger every interval is a thousand light years. Look at him there on the altar. The image is man-made, a little contraption of copper only four feet high. But Shiva-Nataraja fills the universe, is the universe. Shut your eyes and see him towering into the night, follow the boundless stretch of those arms and the wild hair infinitely flying. Nataraja at play among the stars and in the atoms. But also," he added, "also at play within every living thing, every sentient creature, every child and man and woman. Play for play's sake. But now the playground is conscious, the dance floor is capable of suffering. To us, this play without purpose seems a kind of insult. What we would really like is a God who never destroys what he has created. Or if there must be pain and death, let them meted out by a

God of righteousness, who will punish the wicked and reward the good with everlasting happiness. But in fact, the good get hurt, the innocent suffer. Then let there be a God who sympathizes and brings comfort. But Nataraja only dances. His play is a play impartially of death and of life, of all evils as well as of all gods. In the uppermost of his right hands he holds the drum that summons being out of not-being. Rub-a-dub-dub- the creation tattoo, the cosmic reveille. But now look at the uppermost of his left hands. It brandishes the fire by which all that has been created is forthwith destroyed. He dances this way——what happiness! Dances that way——and oh, the pain, the hideous fear, the desolation! Then hop, skip and jump. Hop into perfect health. Skip into cancer and senility. Jump out of the fullness of life into the nothingness, out of nothingness again into life. For Nataraja it's all play, and the play is an end in itself, everlastingly purposeless. He dances because he dances, and the dancing is his maha-sukha, his infinite and eternal bliss. Eternal Bliss," Dr. Robert repeated and again, but questioningly, "Eternal Bliss?" He shook his head. "For us there's no bliss, only the oscillation between happiness and terror and a sense of outrage at the thought that our pains are as integral a part of Nataraja's dance as our pleasures, our dying as our living. Let's quietly think about that for a little while."

The seconds passed, the silence deepened. Suddenly, startlingly, one of the girls began to sob. Vijaya left his place, and kneeling down beside her, laid a hand on her shoulder. The sobbing died down.

"Suffering and sickness," Dr. Robert resumed at last, "old age, decrepitude, death. I show you sorrow. But that wasn't the only thing the Buddha showed us. He also showed us the ending of sorrow."

"Shivayanama," the old priest cried triumphantly.

"Open your eyes again and look at Nataraja up there on the altar. Look closely. In his upper right hand, as you've already seen, he holds the drum that calls the world into existence, and in his upper left hand he carried the destroying fire. Life and death, order and disintegration, impartially. But now look at Shiva's other pair of hands. The lower right hand is raised and the palm is turned outwards. What does that gesture signify? It signifies, 'Don't be afraid; it's All Right.' But how can anyone in his senses fail to be afraid? How can anyone pretend that evil and suffering are all right, when it's so obvious that they're all wrong?

"Nataraja has the answer. Look now at his left hand. He's using it to point down at his feet. And what are his feet doing? Look closely and you'll see the right foot is planted squarely on a horrible little subhuman creature—the demon, Muyalaka. A dwarf, but

191

immensely powerful in his malignity, Muyalaka is the embodiment of ignorance, the manifestation of greedy, possessive selfhood. Stamp on him, break his back! And that's precisely what Nataraja is doing. Trampling the little monster down under his right foot. But notice that it isn't at this trampling right foot that he points his finger; it's at the left foot, the foot that, as he dances, he's in the act of raising from the ground. And why does he point at it? Why? That lifted foot, that dancing defiance of the force of gravity——it's the symbol of release, of moksha, of liberation. Nataraja dances in all the worlds at once——in the world of physics and chemistry, in the world of ordinary, all-too-human experience, in the world finally of Suchness, of Mind, of the Clear Light. And now," Dr. Robert went on after a moment of silence, "I want you to look at the other statue, the image of Shiva and the Goddess. Look at them there in their little cave of light. And now shut your eyes and see them again—— shining, alive, glorified. How beautiful! And in their tenderness what depths of meaning! What wisdom beyond all spoken wisdoms in that sensual experience of spiritual fusion and atonement! Eternity in love with time. The One joined in marriage to the many, the rel-ative made absolute by its union with the One. Nirvana identified with samsara, the manifestation in time and flesh and feeling of the Buddha Nature."

"Shivayanama." The old priest lighted another stick of incense and softly, in a succession of long-drawn melismata, began to chant something in Sanskrit. On the young faces before him Will could read the marks of a listening serenity, the hardly perceptible, ecstatic smile that welcomes a sudden insight, a revelation of truth or of beauty. In the background, meanwhile, Murugan sat wearily slumped against a pillar, picking his exquisitely Grecian nose.

"Liberation," Dr. Robert began again, *"the ending of sorrow, ceasing to be what you ignorantly think you are and becoming what you are in fact. For a little while, thanks to the moksha-medicine, you will know what it's like to be what in fact you are, what in fact you have always been. What a timeless bliss! But, like everything else, this timelessness is transient. Like everything else, it will pass. And when it has passed, what will you do with this experience? What will you do with all the other similar experiences that the moksha-medicine will bring you in the years to come? Will you merely enjoy them as you would enjoy an evening at the puppet show, and then go back to business as usual, back to behaving like the silly delinquents you imagine yourselves to be? Or, having glimpsed, will you devote your lives to the business, not at all as usual, of being what you are in fact? All that we*

older people can do with our teachings, all that . . .
we . . . can do for you with social arrangements, is to
provide you with techniques and opportunities. And
all that the moksha-medicine can do is to give you
a succession of beatific glimpses, an hour or two,
every now and then, of enlightening and liberating
grace. It remains for you to decide whether you'll
co-operate with the grace and take those opportuni-
ties. But that's for the future. Here and now, all you
have to do is to follow. . . [this] advice: Attention!
Pay attention and you'll find yourselves, gradually
or suddenly, becoming aware of the great primordial
facts behind these symbols on the altar."

"Shivayanama!" The old priest waved his stick of
incense. At the foot of the altar steps the boys and
girls sat motionless as statues.

(*Island*, by Aldous Huxley)

This was roughly the same script SLB handed God the next day after their talk about what to do with humans. But the story is the story of the wisdom of the Gods being learned by human beings who pay attention to the obvious, rather than concepts about the obvious. We have the capacity to avoid reality by hiding the obvious behind a concept or memory about it. We learn, for a long time in our lives, how to distort reality, avoid reality, attempt to control reality, enhance reality, program reality, ignore reality—and reality remains hidden from us. We must try for years to do so, finally despair of all attempts to control reality and then in that surrender acknowledge reality and appreciate it in contrast to the struggles and models for control we have spent all that energy creating. We then see, suddenly, the secret of the obvious about how we all function. The best place to hide from experience is behind a concept about that experience. If you want to hide love, hide it behind a concept of love. If you want to hide peace, hide it behind and ideal of peace, etc.

You may think I make too light of things, and God doesn't care much. Well, he doesn't care much and he doesn't waste much. He cares infinitely. He dances because he dances. Well, again, I wish you well, and I hope you understand. But if not, what the hell? What are humans for anyway? It's scary as hell, isn't it? There is no rescue from enlightenment now. I'm crazy because it came on too fast and there is no way back. I don't wish to contribute further to the delinquency of others. Good luck to you. Be careless. —P.H.

• • •

The letter was infuriating and disappointing to me. At the same time I liked very much what he said in the letter and, in fact, wanted to publish that—but it was a letter denying me permission to publish anything! While I was still angry and inspired I got to work trying to do something about it. I put down the letter and made a number of phone calls. I found the hospital he had moved to after his trip to Israel, and since it was close to New York, I called and left a message that I was coming and I went there. I was intending, come hell or high water, to argue, plead, cajole, force or somehow persuade him to let me publish this book. I was treated to yet another enigmatic encounter.

He greeted me with a smile and shook my hand warmly. Then he led me down a series of corridors into his large, carpeted, but simply furnished quarters. A desk, a few books, a couch—and there in the middle of the desk lay the copy of the manuscript I had sent him. He directed me to a chair in front of the desk and indicated that I was to look through the manuscript. The only editorial changes he had made were in the talk-show portion of the book. In the version I had sent him, the names of the discussants were "Dr. Myerson, "Cavett" and "Dr. Howard." He had carefully marked through every instance of the occurrence of "Dr. Howard." and printed "Peter" instead. This is an editorial change which I accepted, as you may have already noticed. The informal reference to him seemed somehow more fitting. Under the influence of his silence, I nodded agreement to the changes and he handed me the already signed permission forms. I must have looked utterly bewildered. He smiled and patted me on the back. He had changed his mind. By way of explanation, he took up a well-used copy of *The Collected Works of D.H. Lawrence*, tore out four pages, folded the last page and tore it carefully in two, put the last page at the beginning and handed me exactly three and three-quarters pages of poem. I accepted the gift.

Without speaking (or having spoken) a word, he took my hand and giggling slightly, led me back down the corridor to the exit. Then someone unlocked the door and let me out.

Peter wasn't working at the hospital as a doctor, he was a patient there—a kind of special patient—but a patient nevertheless. I found out later that he had hurried me along a bit because it was almost three o'clock. Time to go over to Vocational Rehabilitation, where, the hospital staff told me, they had established their only contacts with him through his enthusiasm for learning to sculpt in modeling clay.

The staff said that from 3:00p.m. until 5:00p.m. he worked on making an almost perfect statue of some dancing figure, and then at 5:00 P.M. each day, he would roll his work back into a neat round ball of modeling clay, making it into a kind of globe with all the continents showing. Then, placing it in the center of his table would stand up giggling, and shuffle back to his room.

Everyone on staff was interested in this patient's strange behavior, except they had trouble understanding why he just kept making the same statue over and over and over, day after day, never speaking.

Here is the poem Peter gave me. It was written by D.H. Lawrence and reorganized somewhat by Peter.

A NEW HEAVEN AND A NEW EARTH
D. H. Lawrence

And so I cross into another world
shyly and in homage linger for invitation
from this unknown that I would trespass on.

I am very glad, and all alone in the world,
all alone, and very glad, in a new world
where I am a disembarked at last.
I could cry with joy, because I am in the new
world, just ventured in.
I could cry with joy, and quite freely, there
is nobody to know.
And whosoever the unknown people of this unknown
world may be
they will never understand my weeping for joy to be
adventuring among them
because it will still be a gesture of the old world
I am making
which they will not understand, because it is quite,
quite foreign to them.

II

I was so weary of the world,
I was so sick of it,
everything was tainted with myself,
skies, trees, flowers, birds, water,
people, houses, streets, vehicles, machines,
nations, armies, war, peace-talking,
work, recreation, governing, anarchy,
it was all tainted with myself, I knew it all to
start with because it was all myself.

When I gathered flowers, I knew it was myself
plucking my own flowering.
When I went in a train, I knew it was myself traveling
by my own invention.
When I heard the cannon of the war, I listened with
my own ears to my own destruction.
When I saw the torn dead, I knew it was my own torn
dead body.
It was all me, I had done it all in my own flesh.

III

I shall never forget the maniacal horror of it all in
the end when everything was me, I knew it all already,
I anticipated it all in my soul
because I was the author and the result.
I was God and the creation at once;
creator, I looked at my creation,
created, I looked at myself, the creator;
it was a maniacal horror in the end.

I was lover, I kissed the woman I loved,
And God of horror, I was kissing also myself.
I was the father and a begetter of children,
And oh, oh horror, I was begetting and conceiving
in my own body.

IV

At last came death, sufficiency of death,
and that at last relieved me, I died.
I buried my beloved; it was good, I buried myself and
was gone.
War came, and every hand raised to murder;
very good, very good, every hand raised to murder!
Very good, very good, I am a murderer!
It is good, I can murder and murder, and see them fall,
the mutilated, horror-struck youths, a multitude
one on another, and then in clusters together
smashed, all oozing with blood, and burned in heaps
going up in a fetid smoke to get rid of them,
the murdered bodies of youths and men in heaps
the heaps and heaps and horrible reeking heaps
till it is almost enough, till I am reduced perhaps;
thousands and thousands of gaping, hideous fouled dead
that are youths and men and me
being burned with oil, and consumed in corrupt thick
smoke,
that rolls and taints and blackens the sky, till at last it is
dark,
dark as night, or death, or hell
and I am dead, and trodden to nought in the smoke-
sodden tomb;
dead and trodden to nought in the sour black earth

of the tomb; dead and trodden to nought, trodden to
nought.

V

God, but it is good to have died and been trodden out,
trodden to nought in sour, dead earth,
quite to nought,
absolutely nothing
nothing
nothing
nothing.

For when it is quite, quite nothing, then it is everything.
When I am trodden quite out, quite out,
every vestige gone, then I am here
risen, and setting my foot on another world
risen, accomplishing a resurrection
risen, not born again, but risen, body the same as before.
Now beyond knowledge of newness, alive beyond life,
proud beyond inkling or furthest conception of pride,
living where life was never yet dreamed of, nor hinted at,
here, in the other world, still terrestrial
myself, the same as before, yet unaccountably new.

VI

I, in the sour black tomb, trodden to absolute death
I put out my hand in the night, one night, and my hand
touched that which was verily not me,
verily it was not me.
Where I had been was a sudden blaze,
a sudden flaring blaze!

So I put my hand out further, a little further
and I felt that which was not I,
it verily was not I,
it was the unknown.

Ha, I was a blaze leaping up!
I was a tiger bursting into sunlight.
I was greedy, I was made for the unknown.
I, new-risen, resurrected, starved from the tomb,
starved from a life of devouring always myself,
now here was I, new-awakened, with my hand stretching
out
and touching the unknown, the real unknown, the
unknown unknown

My God, but I can only say
I touch, I feel the unknown!
I am the first comer!

Cortes, Pisarro, Columbus, Cabot, they are nothing,
nothing!
I am the first comer!
I am the discoverer!
I have found the other world!

The unknown, the unknown!
I am thrown upon the shore.
I am covering myself with the sand.
I am filling my mouth with the earth.
I am burrowing my body into the soil.
The unknown, the new world!

VII

It was the flank of my wife
I touched with my hand, I clutched with my hand,
rising, new-awakened from the tomb!
It was the flank of my wife
whom I married years ago
at whose side I have lain for over a thousand nights
and all that previous while, she was I, she was I;
I touched her, it was I who touched and I who was
touched.

Yet rising from the tomb, from the black oblivion
stretching out my hand, my hand flung like a drowned

man's hand on a rock,

I touched her flank and knew I was carried by the

current in death

over to the new world, and was climbing out

on the shore,

risen, not to the old world, the old, changeless I,

the old life,

wakened not to the old knowledge

but to a new earth, a new I, a new knowledge, a new world

of time.

Ah no, I cannot tell you what it is, the new world.

I cannot tell you the mad, astounded rapture of its

discovery.

I shall be mad with delight before I have done,

and whosoever comes after me will find me in the new

world

a madman in rapture.

Peter Howard was, as perhaps all great gurus have been, a madman in rapture. It is my greatest wish that Peter's message, the message of that poem and the message of this book are mirrors of each other. And that looking in these mirrors, we see ourselves. God Bless You.

Brad Blanton, Ph.D.

PUBLISHER'S POSTSCRIPT

BRAD BLANTON doesn't exist. Brad Blanton is a pseudonym for Dr. Victor Myerson. Dr. Myerson became convinced that the best format to present the story of Peter Howard was to adopt a fictitious second personality as editor. He finally understood schizophrenia as an effective form of communication. Early in the writing of the book Peter Howard approved of this idea, saying, at the time, "it turns out we are all eternal split-second sound-light beings anyway, so what's all the fuss about how we label ourselves in order to speak?"

ONE

One Life——
and the myriad interwoven prismatic reflections
intricately moving in place
One Love——
condensing into the infinite
singularities:
these mysteries of individualities
One Light——
awakening inside spheres of rapidly vibrating substances:
rings–pass–not
capturing the uniqueness of the
Self–made selves.
Is there an explanation for this?
Perhaps only that all our joys
and all our sorrows are
a single flower
whose root lies buried in
the heart of the sky
The night and the day being
at one in the origin of the two
and the lighted mind being wedded forever
to the darkness of the still–unknown:
the only certain name
remaining to any of us is. . .
Longing

There
where the past was
memory is better than nothing at all
But the arrow Now
points only beyond itself
and ever and always
beyond any "this" or "here"
The point then. . .
is what will come
and how we will be together in
the as-yet-unmanifested
Inevitable
And when that "then" is "now"
we will be
who? and where?
Space is malleable
and Time no clock:
we will breathe
into beautiful shapes
these forms of
Life and Light and Love
which are to come
All minds and hearts and hands
now fashion the chalices
build the patterns
and carefully assemble
the multidimensional
circuitries
Shall we then be beings

of utmost

innermost

kindliness?

Shall we

in the communion of fearless spirits

build

beautiful worlds?

Shall we become

mutually appreciative

radiant personas

whose masks hide

nothing

but Love itself?

Life says: YES

LABOR FOR THIS

Because there is only the

One-and-the-ones

Creation is a singleness

refracted

a vast Unity and

The Self-same unity

multiplied discrete particular

There is only one

number here

Counting means . . .

counting how many ones

One makes

And what of all

our accountings

of ourselves and others?
These are One Voice
Who then
shall we belittle–
who shall we magnify?
To whom shall we
explain and defend
ourselves——
we
whose very name is. . .
The Unfinished One?

—Diane Harvey